The Weavers

Brad L Raby

Copyright

I with a smile dedicate this to my dear wife who inspired this story. "I wonder if we are even Real", she would ask more than once.

"You knew," she said. Not a question.

"How it would go," he said. "Roughly. The broad strokes." He reeled in his line a little and let it back. "The characters always surprise you, if you're doing it right."

"Did I surprise you."

Chapter 1

CHAPTER ONE: What She Hears at the Edge (revised)

Sarah Mitchell woke at three in the morning on a Tuesday in late February and lay in the dark beside Daniel listening to something she could not quite catch.

Not sound exactly. The quality of sound — the texture of laughter heard through a wall from a room where people are having a very good time and don't know you're listening. Warm. Specific. Gone the moment she turned toward it, the way dreams dissolved when you reached for them, leaving only the feeling of having been somewhere important and the inability to say where.

The cabin settled around her. A board creaked somewhere in the wall. Wind brushed the siding. The cold pressed quietly against the windows. Daniel's breathing beside her was slow and even, the steady rhythm of someone deep in sleep while the house did its quiet winter work.

She felt the thing behind her sternum that had been arriving in small increments for some time now without announcing itself. Not the compass. Not the warning. Something she didn't have a name for yet — with the quality of anticipation in it, the warmth of something approaching that she had been moving toward without realizing she was moving.

It wasn't frightening. That was what she kept returning to in the dark.

The warmth of it.

The almost-laughter of it.

The sense that whatever lived at the edge of hearing regarded her with something very close to affection — the way you might watch someone you have known for a long time, waiting for them to finally do the thing you always suspected they could do.

She reached for it and it was gone.

She lay in the dark and breathed and let it be gone, and after a while she slept.

She dreamed of the river.

Not the December river, not the before-dawn cold of standing in the full version of it, not the immensity arriving like a tide. This was softer — the river in a season she couldn't name, the light different, the water moving with the quiet certainty of something that had been moving for a very long time.

She stood at her bank, the place where the path opened through the willows and the light fell differently than anywhere else along that stretch of water.

And she was not alone.

Someone was there. Downstream, far enough away that looking directly would end the dream, and she wasn't ready for the dream to end.

So she didn't look.

She felt them instead — the way she felt the circle on Thursday nights, the way she felt Daniel's hand in hers in the dark without needing to see it. The presence of another person, warm and particular, unmistakably themselves. Old and young at the same time in a way that made no logical sense and yet felt entirely true.

She stood in the dream river and let the feeling be what it was.

The quiet warmth of someone who knew her.

Someone who found something about this moment — about her standing in the river and finally recognizing the scale of herself — quietly delightful.

Then the February dark came back and Daniel was breathing beside her and the dream was gone.

She lay there for a long time.

Outside the window the first pale beginning of morning was gathering at the tree line, reluctant and grey. She listened for the warmth at the edge of hearing.

Nothing.

Just the cabin. Just the cold. Just Daniel breathing beside her and the quiet fact of the river through the bare trees, moving in the February dark whether she stood in it or not.

She got up and made coffee.

He found her at the kitchen counter when he came in, both hands around her mug, looking out the window where the pale morning was making its slow case for itself against the February grey.

He poured his coffee and stood beside her, leaning lightly against the counter, waiting.

Over the past year — Thursday nights in the barn, river mornings, long drives through December snow — she had come to understand something about Daniel: his waiting was itself a form of presence. The making-room quality of him extended even to silence. Especially to silence.

"The river," she said.

"Yes."

"Someone was there. Downstream." She held the mug between her palms. "I didn't look directly. I just felt them."

"Felt them how?"

She considered that carefully, the way she considered things that mattered — not rushing toward language, letting the right words arrive.

"The way I feel the group on Thursday nights," she said. "Each of them distinct. Warm." She paused. "Like that. But older somehow. Like someone who's been somewhere a long time and finds it —"

She stopped.

"Finds it what?" Daniel said.

She looked out the window. The pale grey light. The bare trees doing their patient winter work.

"Entertaining," she said finally. "Not cruelly. The way you find something entertaining when you love it. When you've been watching it for a long time and it keeps exceeding what you expected."

Daniel stood beside her quietly, making room for that the way he made room for everything — carefully, without pushing, expanding just enough to hold whatever arrived.

"Will they come back?" he said. "In the dream."

"I think so," she said. "I think they've been there for a while and I'm only just starting to hear them."

They stood together in the February kitchen while the morning slowly assembled itself outside the window.

Neither of them tried to name what she had felt downstream. They had both learned something in the barn about the way certain things arrived — that the full version of them came in their own time, and the appropriate response was not to reach but simply to be reachable.

"Thursday," he said.

"Thursday."

Outside the window the February morning continued its quiet negotiation with the day. The light strengthened by degrees. The bare trees held their places with the patience of things that understood warmth was coming and that waiting for it was not the same as being without it.

Sarah held her coffee and felt the thing behind her sternum — the new thing, the not-yet-named thing — and underneath it, faint and warm and entirely certain of itself, the quality of almost-laughter at the very edge of what she could hear.

She didn't reach for it.

She let it stay at the edge.

It would come closer when it was ready.

It had been patient this long.

So could she.

Chapter 2

CHAPTER TWO: Small Things

March arrived the way it always arrived in northern Michigan — not as a season so much as an argument.

The cold refused to concede entirely. Daylight gained by minutes while the temperature ignored the calendar and did what it pleased. The snow was losing, but it wasn't finished yet, and the landscape had the particular quality of something in negotiation with itself — neither what it had been nor what it was becoming.

The bare trees stood in it with their usual patience.

The small things began in the first week.

Robert mentioned the coffee maker on a Thursday night, almost as an aside, the way you mention something that has been sitting in the back of your mind for days and finally finds a moment to come forward.

He had been talking about something else entirely — the January light, the way it had changed for him since the barn, the quality of ordinary mornings now compared to ordinary mornings before — and then he stopped and said,

"My coffee maker turned itself on Tuesday."

The circle waited.

"Before my alarm. Before I was awake. At exactly the time I would have wanted coffee if I'd been awake to want it."

He said it with a small smile — not disbelief exactly, not certainty either. The smile of a man who had been in enough unusual situations lately that the difference between coincidence and something else had become... textured.

Rachel said, "Did it make it right?"

Robert said, "Perfect."

The laughter arrived easily.

Nobody filed it under nothing.

Rachel took a wrong turn on a Wednesday afternoon that she couldn't account for.

She knew the roads between the clinic and her apartment the way you knew roads you drove every day — not consciously, just bodily, the turns happening before you decided to make them.

So the left she took onto a county road she didn't recognize wasn't a decision so much as a fact she discovered after it happened.

The road flattened into open farmland, the wide quiet spaces of agricultural Michigan in late winter.

She drove for a few minutes before she thought to turn around.

In those minutes she passed a barn.

Set back from the road at the end of a dirt track. Old timber construction. A cupola along the ridge. Light in the high windows in the late afternoon grey.

Not Marcus's barn.

Different county. Different trees.

But the same feeling.

The same warmth in the windows.

The same quiet frequency she had been learning to recognize for months.

She pulled over and sat in her car with the engine running.

Looked at the light.

Felt the thing behind her sternum shift slightly — the way a compass shifts when it finds north without being asked.

Then she drove on.

She didn't tell anyone.

But she thought about it for days.

Emma was working late on a Thursday evening — not the Thursday of the gathering, the Thursday before — when the staircase problem finally broke.

She had been circling it for two days.

The load-bearing issue in the community center plans kept resolving technically and failing intuitively, which was the difference that eleven years of grey had cost her and the barn had returned.

She pushed back from her desk and went to the kitchen for coffee.

When she came back the solution was on the plans.

In her handwriting.

Not approximate.

Elegant.

The kind of solution that made other architects stop and look twice.

She stood there for a moment.

Looked at the plans.

Looked at her hand.

Then she picked up her pen and added a small refinement — now that she could see the path, the next step was obvious.

Better.

Undeniably better.

She sat back in her chair.

The office was quiet.

She could feel something moving again in her that had been gone for eleven years — the part of her that worked ahead of her, that solved things while she was making coffee, that left answers waiting in her own handwriting like a message sent across a distance she was only beginning to understand.

"Okay," she said softly to the empty office.

She filed it under:

the barn is working.

David noticed the anomalies in the Meridian documentation on a Monday morning in the second week of March.

He noticed things the way he noticed most things — without alarm, but with the quiet attention of a man who had spent eleven years learning that the most important information rarely announced itself loudly.

An operative named Chen had filed a report on February twenty-eighth.

Three days later the same operative filed an amended report contradicting the first on three specific points.

Not clerical errors.

Interpretations.

The first report described the group as *anomalously cohesive.*

The second used the phrase *unclear.*

In one place the operative had written:

the instruments may not be adequate to the situation.

David read that line three times.

He made a copy.

Filed it.

Then he noticed the surveillance schedule altered without notation — a Thursday night removed entirely from late February.

And a budget line that had existed in January and was gone in February.

No transfer.

No reallocation.

Just gone.

Each thing was small.

Each thing explainable.

Together they had a weight that was beginning to resemble pattern.

David closed the folder.

He said nothing to the group yet.

Information was not the same thing as understanding.

He was waiting for the second.

Marcus went to the river one morning in the last week of February.

The ice had begun pulling back from the banks and the water ran clear and dark beneath it.

He stood at his place — the bank where the path opened through the willows — and felt the frequency the way he always felt it.

Not the expansion Sarah carried.

His was different.

The making-room version.

The chair-setting version.

The quiet patience of a man who had been preparing a space for fourteen years and had only recently discovered that the space had begun filling itself.

He looked downstream.

An old man sat on a rock perhaps forty yards away.

Fishing.

A thermos beside him.

The stillness of him was what Marcus noticed first.

Not the stillness of someone waiting for fish.

There was no waiting in it.

It was the stillness of someone who was exactly where he intended to be and found this entirely sufficient.

Marcus watched him for a while.

Almost called out.

Something stopped him.

Not uncertainty.

Something else.

The quiet sense that calling out would be the wrong instrument for whatever this was.

That voice belonged to a different register than the one this morning occupied.

He watched until the light shifted and the cold in his feet began to insist on itself.

When he looked again the rock was empty.

The old man gone.

The thermos gone.

Just the river and the rock and the pale light moving across the water.

Marcus stood there a moment longer.

Then he turned and walked back up the path.

Something had been placed in the part of him where he kept things without names.

On the last Thursday of the month the group gathered.

The small things came out naturally in the circle — not evidence, not argument.

Just the week's weather.

Robert's coffee maker.

Rachel's wrong turn.

Emma's staircase solution written while she was making coffee.

The group received each one the way they had begun receiving most things lately — not trying to explain them, just holding them for a moment to see what shape they might take.

James looked down at his hands.

Said quietly,

"It's starting."

Emma said, "What is?"

He looked around the circle.

At all of them.

The people he had come back from Pittsburgh for.

The people who had been in the room the night the covered thing finally uncovered.

And said,

"Whatever comes next."

The barn held this.

The stove ticked softly as it cooled.

Outside the late winter cold continued its slow work of becoming March.

Inside the frequency moved through all of them the way it always moved — warm, particular, entirely certain of itself.

And if something in it was slightly warmer than it had been the week before —

Slightly closer.

Slightly more like the texture of laughter heard through a wall from a room where people were having a very good time —

Nobody said so.

But nobody filed it under nothing.

Chapter 3

CHAPTER THREE: The Grocery Store

She almost didn't go.

The list was short enough that she could have sent Daniel, or waited until Saturday when she usually went, or made do with what was in the cabin for another day. But something moved her out the door on a Wednesday afternoon in early March with her keys in her hand and no urgency she could name.

Not decision exactly.

Direction.

The sky was doing the thing it did in early March in northern Michigan — the grey holding a kind of consideration, as if the weather were weighing its options and hadn't decided yet.

She drove with the radio off.

The quiet suited her. The thing behind her sternum — the new thing, the not-yet-named thing — had become a kind of companion now. Warm. Patient. Present at the edge of everything.

The cereal aisle was empty.

Wednesday afternoons had that quality — the store suspended between its busy hours, the fluorescent lights doing their indifferent work overhead.

She reached for her usual brand.

The one she'd been buying for years without thinking.

Her hand stopped.

Not dramatically.

No warning.

Just — stopped, the way a foot stops at the edge of a step in the dark. Some part of her operating slightly ahead of her conscious attention, finding something that required a pause.

She stood there with her hand in the air.

At the far end of the aisle a woman with a cart was watching her with the mild concern people reserve for strangers behaving oddly in grocery stores.

Sarah lowered her hand.

Looked at the shelf.

Reached one row to the left and took a different box — a brand she'd never bought, a little more expensive, no reason she could think of.

She put it in her cart and walked on.

By the time she drove back toward the cabin she had nearly convinced herself it meant nothing.

Which was itself a kind of evidence.

The things that mattered most always seemed to require the most convincing away from.

She set the box on the counter.

Daniel looked at it the way he looked at small unexpected things — with the full, unhurried attention of someone who had learned that small unexpected things were often the interesting ones.

"You changed brands," he said.

"I don't know why."

He looked at her for a moment.

"But you knew to."

She looked at the box again.

"My hand stopped," she said. "And then it didn't."

Daniel nodded slowly.

That was enough.

She opened the box.

Lifted the wax paper.

Found the card.

Small. Promotional. A loyalty code — numbers and letters arranged in a sequence that meant nothing to her, the sort of thing she would normally drop into the recycling without reading.

She looked at it.

Then held it out to Daniel.

He took it.

His stillness shifted — the making-room quiet becoming something sharper.

"That's the address format David uses," he said.

"For facility documentation."

"Yes."

They stood together in the kitchen looking at the card while the ordinary afternoon light moved through the window and the bare trees outside did nothing in particular.

At the very edge of hearing she felt the warmth again.

Closer now.

Watching.

She called David.

He answered on the second ring, the way he always did when her name appeared.

She read him the code.

The pause on the other end of the phone was the particular pause of David encountering something his framework was not prepared for.

She had heard it before.

"That's the address of the Indiana facility," he said.

She set the card down on the table.

"The one Robert was in."

"Yes."

She looked at the card again.

At the kitchen.

At the ordinary Wednesday afternoon arranged around this small impossible thing.

"How," she said.

Not really a question.

"I don't know," David said.

And the honesty of it settled into the room with its own kind of weight.

After she hung up she stood at the table for a long time.

And at the edge of hearing — closer than it had ever been, warm and unmistakably deliberate — something moved through the room.

Not quite laughter.

Not quite not laughter.

A shift in the air.

Present for a moment.

Gone again.

Leaving the kitchen slightly different than it had been.

Not frightening.

Patient.

That was the word that kept returning.

Patient.

She picked up her pen and wrote on the notepad by the phone.

The card. The facility address. Someone left it for me to find.

She paused.

Then added another line.

They've been leaving things for a while. I'm only just learning to see them.

She told the group Thursday night.

Not all of them were there yet.

The circle received it the way they had begun receiving things — with quiet attention, nobody rushing toward explanation.

James looked down at his hands.

Emma seemed to measure the shape of it the way she measured structures.

Robert was very still.

Rachel looked at David.

David looked back.

Something moved between them that had been moving for months now, drawing closer to wherever it intended to land.

After a while Marcus said,

"They're interested in us."

Sarah shook her head slightly.

"I think they've always been interested," she said. "I think we're only just becoming interesting enough to notice."

The barn held that.

The stove ticked softly.

Outside the March dark pressed against the high windows.

Inside the frequency moved through the circle the way it always moved — warm, particular, slightly fuller than the week before.

And somewhere in the dim back of the barn, just beyond the reach of the amber light —

Something that might have been presence and might not —

Held its warmth in the shadows.

If anyone had looked directly they would have seen nothing.

Nobody looked.

Sarah felt it.

Both kinds.

She filed it where she kept the things that did not yet have names.

Under:

wait.

Under:

soon.

Chapter 4

CHAPTER FOUR: Meridian Losing Small Things

The building in Indianapolis had been designed to discourage memory.

Long concrete corridors, neutral paint, light from ceiling panels instead of windows — the sort of architecture that made every hallway resemble the last, as though the building preferred not to be remembered in pieces.

Director Voss had worked there for twelve years. She could walk its corridors without looking up from the file in her hand.

Which was what she was doing when the first small thing occurred.

She reached the security door at the end of the corridor and held her key card to the panel.

Nothing happened.

She waited for the familiar click.

The panel remained dark.

She tried again.

Still nothing.

Behind her someone cleared their throat politely — a junior analyst with a stack of folders held carefully against his chest. She stepped aside to let him try.

His card worked immediately.

The lock released with its ordinary mechanical certainty.

The door opened.

Voss walked through without comment.

Inside the secure office area the air carried the faint smell of printer toner and the industrial coffee that appeared in the break room every morning without anyone quite knowing who replaced the pot.

She sat at her desk.

Opened the Chen report.

Read the amended section again.

The instruments may not be adequate to the situation.

It was not the sentence itself that troubled her.

Field agents occasionally reached for language when data refused to behave.

What troubled her was the tone behind it — not alarm, not speculation, but a quiet suggestion that the framework itself might be insufficient.

She closed the report and opened the surveillance schedule.

Thursday nights had been observed for months.

Predictably.

Methodically.

A small group gathering in a rural barn.

Meditation. Discussion. Occasional outdoor activity.

Nothing operationally significant.

The entry for the last Thursday in February was gone.

Not crossed out.

Not archived.

Gone in the particular way that information sometimes disappeared from systems designed specifically to prevent disappearance.

Voss leaned back slightly in her chair.

Not alarmed.

Just attentive.

Experience had taught her that organizations rarely failed dramatically.

They failed in increments.

An assumption here.

A misfiled document there.

One piece of information drifting slightly out of alignment with the others.

She opened the budget file.

A line item present in January did not appear in February.

No transfer.

No reallocation.

Simply absent.

Three small things.

Each one explainable on its own.

Together they carried the faint suggestion of pattern.

She closed the file but did not remove her hand from it immediately.

Information, she reminded herself, was not yet understanding.

Outside her office the quiet machinery of Meridian continued its work.

Phones.

Keyboards.

Footsteps in the hallway.

People moving with the calm confidence of those who believed the systems around them were functioning exactly as intended.

Voss stood and walked toward the break room.

The coffee machine hummed softly.

Someone had left a folded newspaper on the counter.

Near the far wall a janitor was replacing the liner in a waste bin.

He looked older than most of the staff — thin shoulders, grey hair at the temples — the kind of presence that became nearly invisible through familiarity.

Voss poured coffee.

The janitor tied the bag closed and set it in the cart beside him, the wheels squeaking faintly against the tile.

As he turned to leave he said, without looking up,

"You folks keep losing little things."

Voss glanced toward him.

"What things?"

He shrugged.

"Oh, schedules. Numbers." A faint smile crossed his face. "Sometimes that's how it starts."

He wheeled the cart out into the corridor and disappeared around the corner.

Voss stood there a moment longer than necessary.

Not because of the words.

Because of the tone.

It had not sounded like speculation.

It had sounded like recognition.

She returned to her office.

Sat down.

Opened the Chen file again.

The amended report contained a line she had not noticed before.

Subject group exhibits cooperative behavioral patterns inconsistent with expected cohesion models.

She read it twice.

Not wrong.

Just oddly phrased.

As though the agent had been reaching for something and decided midway through the sentence not to finish reaching.

She wrote a note in the margin.

Then another.

Then closed the folder and looked through the glass wall of her office into the hallway beyond.

Somewhere in northern Michigan a small group of people were meeting in a barn on Thursday nights.

They talked.

They sat in silence.

Sometimes they walked down to a river.

None of which, on its face, constituted a threat.

And yet.

Patterns did not require intention to exist.

Sometimes they appeared simply because enough small events began leaning in the same direction.

Voss opened a new document.

Typed a short directive.

Verify surveillance continuity. Confirm system integrity. Initiate secondary observation protocol.

She read it once.

Then sent it.

Not escalation.

Not yet.

Verification.

In Michigan the late winter light was beginning to soften.

Marcus arrived at the barn early Thursday afternoon to light the stove.

The air inside still carried the cold of the morning.

He stacked the kindling.

Lit the fire.

Sat for a moment in one of the chairs and listened to the quiet breathing of the building as it warmed.

The barn had learned the shape of Thursdays.

It seemed to recognize when people were coming.

Marcus stood and opened the door.

Across the clearing the trees remained bare, but at the very tips of their branches something had begun.

A change too small to see clearly.

He noticed it without deciding to notice it.

He walked down the path to the river.

The ice had pulled farther back from the banks now, leaving the water to move dark and steady through the open channel.

He stood there for a while.

Looked downstream.

The rock where he had seen the fisherman earlier in the week was empty.

Just the river.

Just the light moving across the current.

Just the quiet certainty of water continuing where it had always gone.

Marcus smiled slightly.

Not because he understood anything.

Because the world had begun behaving like a story again.

He turned and walked back toward the barn.

Halfway up the path he noticed something that made him pause.

Footprints in the soft mud beside the trail.

Two sets.

One of them his.

The other slightly older, leading down toward the river.

He studied them for a moment.

Then shook his head gently and continued walking.

That evening the circle gathered.

Robert arrived with a loaf of bread he insisted he had baked himself, which Rachel examined with the careful suspicion of someone who suspected the bakery in town might have assisted.

Emma came in carrying a roll of drawings under her arm.

David arrived last, quiet as always.

Chairs moved softly on the wooden floor.

The stove ticked as the iron warmed.

Conversation drifted through the room the way it often did now — easily, without urgency, the group settling into the particular rhythm they had discovered together.

Outside the March dark gathered around the barn.

Inside the frequency moved through them — warm, particular, slightly fuller than it had been the week before.

No one remarked on it.

Not directly.

But more than one person glanced toward the door without quite knowing why.

Later, after the conversation had settled into silence for a while, Marcus stepped outside to bring in another armful of wood.

The clearing was quiet.

The stars had begun appearing above the tree line.

He stacked the wood beside the stove and returned to his chair.

For a moment he thought he heard something from the direction of the river.

Not a sound exactly.

Something closer to the feeling of someone enjoying a joke.

He listened.

Nothing followed.

Marcus sat back down.

Across the room Sarah noticed him smile faintly and wondered what he had heard.

Neither of them said anything.

In Indianapolis, long after the staff had gone home, the Meridian building settled into its night silence.

In Voss's office the surveillance system completed its routine archive cycle.

One camera feed in a rural part of Michigan rotated slightly as it reset its position.

Then it rotated a little farther.

The adjustment was small.

Only a few degrees.

Just enough that the barn it had been observing no longer sat in the center of the frame.

Instead the camera now pointed slightly toward the trees.

The system logged the change automatically.

No alert was triggered.

And if anyone had been watching the monitor at that moment, they might have thought they saw movement among the shadows near the edge of the clearing.

But the camera stabilized again.

The image held steady.

Nothing unusual remained.

Only the quiet barn.

And the trees beyond it.

Somewhere in that darkness someone might have been standing very still, watching the warm light in the barn windows with the quiet satisfaction of a person who had just moved a single piece on a very large board.

Or perhaps no one had been there at all.

The system registered no anomaly.

The night continued.

But the camera never quite returned to its original position.

And in the morning, when Director Voss reviewed the surveillance logs, she paused for a moment longer than usual before moving on.

Not because she knew what she was looking at.

Because she had the faint, unsettling impression that something in the system had just... adjusted itself.

A small thing.

The sort of thing that rarely mattered.

Unless it kept happening.

Chapter 5

CHAPTER FIVE: The Shape of Things

The snow left quietly.

Not all at once, not with the theatrical melt that sometimes came in April, but slowly — the way winter withdrew when it had other places to be. The fields turned from white to the color of wet paper. The edges of the roads softened. The ditches began carrying small thin streams of water that moved with the patient certainty of things that had been waiting under the ice for months.

Sarah noticed the change first in the mornings.

Light arrived earlier now.

The river carried more sound.

Not louder exactly, just fuller — the way a voice sounded when someone had begun saying something but had not yet decided how much of it they intended to say.

She stood on the bank with her hands in the pockets of her coat and listened.

Somewhere upstream something splashed.

A branch shifting in the current perhaps.

Or a fish.

Or nothing in particular.

The river had been teaching her lately that *nothing in particular* was often where the interesting things began.

Behind her on the path Daniel approached, his steps quiet in the damp ground.

"You look like someone waiting for something," he said.

"I might be," she said.

"For what?"

She thought about that.

The water moved steadily past them.

"Confirmation," she said finally.

Daniel nodded as though that made sense.

It did not always matter that he understood what she meant. What mattered was that he understood that she meant something.

They walked back toward the cabin together.

Halfway up the path Sarah stopped.

"What?" Daniel asked.

She frowned slightly and looked toward the trees behind them.

"I thought someone was there."

Daniel turned.

The trees stood quietly in the late morning light. Bare branches. A few patches of snow lingering in the shadows.

Nobody.

"What did it feel like?" he said.

She considered.

"Friendly," she said.

Then she laughed softly.

"Which is an odd thing to say about someone who may not exist."

Daniel smiled.

"I've noticed the same thing," he said.

They kept walking.

Neither of them mentioned the sound of gravel shifting lightly behind them as they reached the cabin door.

That evening David arrived at the barn earlier than usual.

Marcus had already lit the stove and the warmth was beginning to push back the chill that still lived in the wooden beams.

David set his coat over the back of a chair and stood for a moment looking around the room.

"You look like someone carrying information," Marcus said.

David smiled faintly.

"That obvious?"

Marcus shrugged.

"Information has a posture."

David sat.

Marcus waited.

After a moment David said, "Meridian has begun asking quiet questions."

Marcus did not appear surprised.

"What kind of questions?"

"Verification," David said. "System checks. Secondary observation."

Marcus nodded slowly.

"Escalation?"

"Not yet."

David leaned forward slightly.

"They don't know what they're escalating toward."

Marcus stirred the fire with the poker.

The wood shifted.

Sparks moved briefly up the chimney.

"That seems fair," Marcus said.

David looked at him.

"You don't sound concerned."

Marcus smiled.

"Concern assumes something is wrong."

David considered that.

"You don't think something is wrong?"

Marcus shook his head.

"I think something is happening."

The door opened.

Rachel came in carrying a bag of groceries and an expression that suggested she had been laughing recently.

"You'll appreciate this," she said, setting the bag on the table.

"What happened?" Marcus said.

"Three cars parked outside the grocery store," she said. "Government plates."

David raised an eyebrow.

Rachel continued.

"They were all parked perfectly. Except one."

"What was wrong with it?" Marcus asked.

"The front end was pointing up," she said.

"Up?"

"Up," Rachel repeated. "Like someone had tried to park it on a telephone pole guy wire."

Marcus laughed.

David did not.

"Nobody hurt?" he asked.

Rachel shook her head.

"Embarrassed, though."

She unpacked the groceries while the others began arriving — Robert with his perpetual loaf of bread, Emma carrying a sketch pad she claimed not to be working on, James moving quietly the way he always did when something in the room mattered to him.

The chairs filled.

Conversation moved around the circle.

Small things.

Weather.

Work.

The way the light had been changing.

And then, naturally, the other things.

Robert's coffee maker.

Emma's staircase solution.

Sarah's cereal box card.

Rachel's oddly parked government vehicle.

The group held each story carefully, the way they had begun holding most things now — not trying to explain them, just letting them exist long enough to see whether they belonged to something larger.

After a while Emma said quietly,

"You ever notice how things keep happening right when they would make the most sense?"

The room was still for a moment.

Marcus tilted his head.

"What do you mean?"

Emma gestured with her pencil.

"Like a story."

Robert grinned.

"If this is a story, whoever's writing it really doesn't like Meridian."

Laughter moved through the room.

David smiled despite himself.

But the thought lingered in the air a moment longer than the joke required.

Marcus leaned back in his chair.

"You think someone is arranging things?"

Emma shrugged.

"Or maybe nudging them."

Rachel looked around the circle.

"Toward what?"

Nobody answered.

Outside the barn the night had settled fully over the clearing.

The river moved quietly through the trees.

Inside the stove ticked as the fire shifted.

And somewhere beyond the edge of the clearing, just out of the light spilling from the barn door, someone might have been standing with his hands in the pockets of a worn coat, listening to the laughter inside with the quiet pleasure of someone who had been hoping a group of people might eventually begin asking the right questions.

Or perhaps the trees were simply moving in the wind.

Inside the barn Marcus added another log to the stove.

The flames rose.

The circle continued.

And far away in Indianapolis Director Voss sat at her desk reading a surveillance update that contained three words she did not like at all.

Observation inconclusive again.

She read the line twice.

Then reached for the phone.

Not escalation yet.

But close.

Very close.

And somewhere, not in Michigan and not in Indiana but in a place that seemed to overlap both slightly, someone closed a small notebook and looked up at the night sky with a satisfied expression.

"That should keep things interesting," he said quietly.

Then he slipped the notebook into his coat pocket and walked down toward the river.

Chapter 6

CHAPTER SIX: Observation Protocol

The order came through quietly.

No alarms.

No red flags.

Just a short directive sent through the Meridian system late on a Thursday afternoon.

Secondary observation protocol authorized. Maintain distance. Record only.

Agent Kline read the message twice.

"Looks like we're watching a book club," he said.

Agent Ortega didn't look up from the equipment case.

"Book clubs don't usually get federal surveillance," she said.

Kline shrugged.

"Everything gets federal surveillance eventually."

They parked the SUV on the narrow county road half a mile from the barn.

The sun was already dropping behind the trees. Late winter light moved across the fields in long flat bands that made the snow look older than it was.

Kline set the drone case on the hood of the vehicle.

Ortega adjusted the small monitoring screen mounted to the dashboard.

"Power?"

"Good."

"Camera?"

"Good."

The drone rose smoothly into the evening air.

On the screen the clearing appeared — the barn sitting exactly where the reports said it would be, warm light beginning to show in the upper windows.

"Looks like people arriving," Ortega said.

The screen showed a car pulling into the clearing.

Then another.

Then someone walking down the path toward the river.

Kline leaned closer to the monitor.

"That the group?"

"Probably."

The drone drifted slightly.

Ortega corrected it.

The camera steadied again.

For several minutes nothing unusual happened.

People entered the barn.

Lights moved inside.

Someone stepped outside briefly and returned with an armful of wood.

Kline leaned back against the seat.

"You ever feel like we're missing something?" he said.

Ortega didn't answer immediately.

She was watching the monitor.

The camera had begun turning slowly.

She adjusted the control stick.

Nothing changed.

The drone continued rotating.

Now the barn slid out of the center of the frame.

The camera pointed toward the trees.

"What's it doing?" Kline said.

Ortega checked the controller.

"I'm correcting it."

The drone continued to turn.

Now the camera faced almost straight up.

The screen filled with sky.

Stars beginning to appear.

Ortega frowned.
"That shouldn't happen."
Kline laughed softly.
"Maybe it wants a better view."
Ortega reset the control program.
The drone stopped rotating.
For a moment it hovered perfectly still.
Then it lowered itself three feet and began drifting gently sideways.
Away from the barn.
"What the hell—"
Ortega grabbed the controls.
The drone continued moving.
Slowly.
Deliberately.
Like something following a path it had already decided on.
The camera turned once more.
Now the screen showed the county road.
Their SUV.
Both agents standing beside it.
Kline stared at the monitor.
"You seeing this?"
"Yes."
The drone hovered for another moment.
Then the motors powered down.
The machine settled carefully into the snow beside the road.
No crash.
No malfunction.
Just a quiet landing.
Ortega walked over and picked it up.
She checked the diagnostics.
Everything read normal.
Battery full.

Motors responsive.
Camera operational.
She looked back toward the barn.
The lights glowed softly through the high windows.
Inside the circle had begun.
Kline shook his head.
"You want to try again?"
Ortega considered.
Then she said, "No."
They packed the drone away.
Sat in the SUV.
Watched the clearing through binoculars instead.
The barn door opened briefly.
Someone stepped out.
Looked toward the trees.
Then returned inside.
Kline rubbed his hands together.
"You think they know we're here?"
Ortega stared at the dark edge of the clearing.
"I think something does."
Half an hour later the agents decided to reposition.
Kline started the SUV.
The engine turned over smoothly.
He shifted into reverse.
The vehicle did not move.
He checked the gear indicator.
Park.
He moved the lever again.
Reverse.
The engine hummed.
The SUV remained perfectly still.
Ortega leaned forward.

"Try drive."

He did.

Nothing.

Kline frowned.

"You got the parking brake?"

"No."

They both stepped out of the vehicle.

The rear wheels were resting against a low ridge of frozen snow.

Barely noticeable.

But enough.

The tires spun slightly when Kline tried the engine again.

The SUV did not move.

He shut it off.

Stared at the ridge.

"We didn't park against that."

Ortega looked toward the barn again.

The lights glowed warmly through the windows.

Inside, faintly, they could hear laughter.

Not loud.

Just enough to reach them across the clearing.

Kline sighed.

"You hear that?"

Ortega nodded.

"Yeah."

He looked down at the tire tracks behind the vehicle.

Then back toward the barn.

"You know what this feels like?"

"What?"

He smiled faintly.

"Like somebody moved the furniture."

Ortega did not answer.

Inside the barn the circle was deep in conversation.

Robert had just finished describing the strange position of the government car he had seen outside the grocery store earlier that day.

Rachel was laughing.

Marcus leaned back in his chair.

"You ever notice how things keep happening right when they would make the most sense?" he said.

Emma raised an eyebrow.

"Meaning?"

Marcus gestured vaguely toward the door.

"Like a story."

Laughter moved through the circle.

Outside the barn the Meridian agents pushed against the SUV again.

The vehicle shifted slightly.

Just enough.

Inside the barn the laughter continued.

And somewhere down by the river, where the current moved steadily through the thinning ice, an old man sat on a rock with a small notebook resting on his knee.

He wrote something slowly.

Read it once.

Then crossed out a word.

"Too obvious," he said quietly.

He looked up toward the barn.

From where he sat he could see the agents beside their vehicle.

He smiled.

Not unkindly.

Then he wrote another line.

The SUV behind the agents rolled forward three inches.

Just enough to free the tire.

Kline stared at it.

"You see that?"

Ortega nodded slowly.

Neither of them mentioned the sound they thought they heard drifting faintly across the river.

Something like quiet laughter.

Or the turning of a page.

Chapter 7

SEEN: WHAT YOU ARE CHAPTER Seven: MAREN

The snow had finally given up its argument with March, sulking away in gray patches at the field's edge the way a losing position sulks — still technically present, making a point of it, fooling no one.

She came through the door on a Thursday night and the barn did what barns don't do, which is settle. Not the creak and pop of cold timber finding warmth. Something else. The specific settling of a space that has been slightly less than itself for some time and has now, without announcement, become the full version.

Nobody saw her come in. That was the first thing. Marcus had been watching the door — habit, the patient courtesy of a man who had been doing this long enough to know that the door was where the night declared its intentions — and the door had not opened in the way doors open when someone comes through them. Yet there she was in the chair that had not been there, getting tea without being shown where the kettle was, with the unhurried ease of someone who has found the kettle in any number of barns.

Grey hair. The kind that had stopped apologizing for itself so long ago the apology wasn't even a memory. Not wild exactly — more like it had made an independent assessment of its situation and decided chaos was the only honest policy. The face underneath it was wrong in the specific way that things are wrong when your framework for them is the problem rather than the thing itself. Young in a way that the hair contradicted and the eyes refused to settle.

Sarah felt it the moment the barn settled.

Not recognition of a face. Recognition of a quality — the warm-laughter-through-a-wall quality she had been reaching for at three in the morning and finding gone the moment she reached. Here now. Present. Sitting across the circle with a mug she'd poured herself, looking at the assembled Thursday people with eyes that were doing several things simultaneously, none of which were introduction.

I know you, she thought.

Across the circle the eyes found hers. Held for one beat, two, the young-ancient thing in them saying something back that had no words in it and needed none. Then moving on, unhurried, to the next person and the next, as if conducting a quiet inventory of something it had been expecting to find and was pleased to confirm.

Sarah looked at her tea.

Marcus, who had been building spaces for people to find themselves for long enough to have developed genuine patience with the unprecedented, said: "I don't think we've met."

Maren looked at him with the attention of someone who has been handed a puzzle they intend to enjoy at their own pace. Something in the look was warm. Something in it was also, faintly, amused — not at Marcus but at the whole situation, the whole room, the whole ongoing project of human beings finding each other in barns on Thursday nights and calling it a coincidence.

"You have excellent chairs," she said.

She drank her tea and looked at the high windows where the March dark pressed against the old glass, and the circle continued the way circles do when a new element has been introduced that everyone is still calibrating — a shade more careful, a shade more present, the frequency in the room finding a new register the way a tuning fork finds its note when you strike it against something true.

She didn't explain herself. She listened. Not the listening of someone waiting for their turn to speak — the listening of someone who already knows the story and has come for the quality of the telling, for the specific texture of these particular people working their way toward things she has been watching people work toward for considerably longer than anyone in this barn would find comfortable to estimate.

Robert was talking about the light he'd been seeing — not dramatically, the way people talk about visions, but the way he talked about everything now, with the careful specificity of a man who had come back from somewhere far away and found that precision was the best available courtesy to the truth. The quality at the edge of things. The way certain people's hands looked in certain light. Maren listened to this with the focused attention she'd given nothing else all evening, and when he finished she looked into her mug for a moment, and then looked at him directly.

Something passed between them in the looking. Robert held it without flinching, which said something about how far he'd come.

She nodded once. Not in the way of agreement — in the way of confirmation. Of a thing recognized.

Then she looked away and the moment closed and the circle moved on and nobody asked what the nod had meant because the barn had been teaching them, Thursday by Thursday, that some things landed better when you let them sit.

Rachel was talking about the cars. The black sedans at the end of the road — the slow, institutional patience of them, the way they sat without moving for an hour and then were simply gone, no engine sound, no visible departure. The group's familiar dance with this information: David's procedural calm, Emma's architectural attention to the pattern of it, James's compressed anger that still hadn't found its full outlet.

Maren listened to this differently. Not with the confirmation she'd given Robert. With the sharpened attention of someone who has seen this particular staging from the other side of the theater many times and has developed considered opinions about how it ends. Her mug lowered slightly. Her eyes went briefly to the high windows — not nervous, not alarmed, the reflexive check of someone accounting for exits not for their own sake but out of long habit.

Then the attention released and she drank her tea and the circle went on.

At some point she said, into a pause between Emma finishing a thought and Daniel beginning one: "The interesting question isn't what they're watching for." She didn't look up from her mug. "It's what they do when they see it."

The circle sat with this for a moment.

"What do they do," Grace asked.

Maren looked up. The young-ancient eyes, patient, the warmth in them unhurried. "Depends on the person," she said. "Some of them figure out what side they're on."

She said nothing else on the subject. The circle moved on. But the barn held the words the way it held everything spoken honestly inside it — present, folded into the frequency, available when needed.

Down at the river, in the cold that the March dark brought to the water's edge, an old man sat on his rock with a small notebook on his knee. The thermos beside him. The line in the water going nowhere productive, which was fine because the fishing wasn't the point.

He wrote something. Read it back. Crossed a word out.

Looked up toward the barn, where the warm light moved in the high windows and the Thursday frequency was running fuller than it had run before tonight.

He wrote another line.

Then he sat for a while not writing, listening to the river work its patient argument with the remaining ice, and felt — with the specific satisfaction of someone watching something unfold precisely as it should while remaining genuinely surprised by the details — that tonight had gone well. Better than the outline, which was always the goal.

He picked up the thermos. Raised it briefly toward the warm windows.

Then he wrote one more thing, crossed that out too, and wrote it again differently, and this time left it.

Between the putting on of coats and the sound of first engines turning over in the cold parking lot, Maren was gone. Her chair was in the circle where it belonged, as if it had always belonged there, which perhaps it had. Her cup was on the table. The kettle was where it lived.

No door sound. No cold draft announcing an exit. No creak of the threshold timber that had been broadcasting departures faithfully for forty years.

Marcus stood in the nearly empty barn and felt the frequency — not diminished by everyone going home, but larger, the way a room feels larger after someone opens a window you didn't know was there. He stood with it for a moment before turning off the lights.

In the car Sarah said, before Daniel could say anything, "She was in the dream."

"The hair," he said.

"Yes."

He drove. The late-March dark, the road they knew, the quiet of two people carrying the same thing in the same direction.

"She already knew us," Sarah said. "Not like meeting. Like checking in."

Daniel was quiet for a moment, the making-room quality of him present in the silence, finding space for it.

"Did she say what she is," he said.

Sarah thought about the nod to Robert. The sharpened attention during Rachel's surveillance report. The single sentence that wasn't quite an answer and wasn't quite not one.

"Not in words," she said.

They drove through the last of March and both of them felt it — the both-and of something arrived that had been expected without knowing it was being expected, the frequency of the barn running behind them in the dark, fuller than it was before Thursday, and whatever came next already gathering itself somewhere just past the edge of what the headlights could reach.

END OF CHAPTER SIX

The key differences from my earlier shorter draft: I've added the Robert confirmation beat, the Rachel/surveillance moment with Maren's theater-veteran attention, her one substantive line about what the watchers do when they see it, and the Old Man at the river with the notebook — borrowed from Chat's chapter where it belongs, which is at the river in the margins, not at the center.

Chapter 8

SEEN: WHAT YOU ARE CHAPTER EIGHT: CARL

Amy had been different for three weeks before he said anything about it.

Not different badly. That was the thing that kept stopping him when he reached for the word wrong, which was the word he'd been carrying toward it since the first Thursday she came home quieter than she left and sat at the kitchen table for twenty minutes just holding her coffee. Not sad quiet. The other kind — the quiet of someone who has set something down they didn't know they were carrying and is noticing the absence of the weight.

He watched this from the doorway and filed it under: wait.

Carl was a man who filed things. Sixty-three years of physical work and raising children and running a business had produced in him a filing system of considerable efficiency and almost no flexibility, which was a combination that had served him well enough that he saw no reason to examine it. Things went into categories. Categories had labels. Labels told you what something was and therefore what to do about it.

Amy's three weeks didn't have a label that fit.

So on a Thursday in late March he drove her, which was how he said it to himself — *I'll drive her* — not *I'll go* and not *I'll see what this is*, because those framings would have required him to admit he was looking for something rather than supervising something, and that was a distinction Carl was not yet prepared to make.

The barn sat in its clearing at the end of the gravel road the way old barns sit — with the particular authority of a structure that has been exactly where it is for long enough that the land has organized itself around it. Carl noted this without sentiment. A well-built thing. Timber frame, properly maintained. He could see from the lot that the foundation was sound.

Inside he took a chair near the back and crossed his arms and conducted his inspection.

The people first. He catalogued them with the practiced efficiency of a man who had been reading rooms his whole life: the big one who'd built the place, patient, the kind of patient that isn't waiting for anything specific; the young woman who laughed easily; the precise man who listened like he was keeping records; the one who'd been somewhere far away and recently returned, you could see it in how carefully he held things. Ordinary people in an old barn on a Thursday night.

Then Maren.

She was already in her chair when he looked, which meant he'd missed her arrival, which was not something Carl typically missed. He looked at her the way he looked at things that needed categorizing — direct, thorough, the full assessment — and found that the assessment kept sliding off without completing itself. Not young. Not old. The hair doing whatever it wanted and apparently having done so for some time. The face suggesting an age and then suggesting something else entirely, and the eyes, when they reached him, doing something that no category he had accommodated before.

He looked away first.

Carl was not a man who looked away first. He noted this, filed it under something he didn't have a label for yet, and recrossed his arms.

She looked at him for one more moment after he'd looked away — he could feel it, the specific quality of someone taking a measurement — and then moved on, and the gathering began, and he sat in the back with his arms crossed and listened to people say things he had no framework for.

Not foolish things. That was also stopping him. He'd come prepared to be patient with foolishness — had driven forty minutes to be patient with it, which was its own kind of love for Amy that he wouldn't have called love. But the people in this circle were not fools.

The precise man spoke about patterns in observable behavior with the care of someone who respected evidence. The big one who'd built the place said almost nothing and when he spoke it landed with the weight of things said by people who don't waste words. Amy sat three chairs to his left and held her coffee with both hands and was the most present version of herself he had seen in years and he could not account for this and could not file it and kept almost reaching for a category and finding the shelf empty.

Maren said very little. When she spoke the barn did what the rafters of old buildings do in shifting weather — a small adjustment, barely audible, the timber finding a new equilibrium. Nobody remarked on it. Carl remarked on it internally and could not explain why a woman saying six words should make a sixty-year-old barn settle differently on its foundation.

He drove home with Amy and said nothing on the way, which was normal, and sat in his own driveway for nineteen minutes after she went inside, which was not.

He went to bed.

The dream came at the depth of the night when the house was fully quiet and his wife was a warm specific weight beside him and the dark was complete.

He was in a room he recognized without knowing where it was, the way you recognize things in dreams before the recognition makes any sense. Full of people. People he knew, had known, from across sixty-three years — not a gathering, not a reunion, just people present the way they actually were rather than the way he'd filed them.

That was the thing. The thing that had no category.

He could feel them.

Not their surfaces, not the versions that fit the labels he'd assigned — difficult, reliable, demanding, useful, manageable — but the actual versions, the full ones, each person present and distinct and considerably larger than the file he'd been keeping on them. A woman he'd worked beside for eleven years whose grief he had catalogued as *emotional, handle with patience* and who in the dream was enormous with it, the grief of a person who had lost the irreplaceable, and he had stood next to that grief for eleven years and called it a management situation.

Near the back of the room stood a man he had not thought about in thirty years.

Not because the man was forgettable. Because Carl had made him forgettable, which was a different thing and worse, and standing in the dream room he understood this with the clean horrible clarity of something true arriving without warning. Not cruelty — he had not been cruel to this man. Crueler than cruelty, the small sustained wrongness of a person reduced to a label that made Carl comfortable and the man small. Filed under: *limited, keep expectations low*, and left there for the length of a working relationship and then not thought of again.

The man in the dream was not accusing him. He was simply there, the full version of himself, and the full version had nothing to do with the file Carl had kept. The full version was a person of considerable interior life and quiet dignity who had spent years in proximity to a man who had decided he wasn't worth the full version of anything.

Carl stood in the dream and felt this with nowhere to put it.

He woke at three in the morning into the dark and the quiet and his wife's breathing beside him.

He could feel her.

Not the fact of her — fifty-one years had made the fact of her as ambient as the house itself, the furniture, the specific creaks of the hallway floor. The actual her. Sleeping. Her weight in the bed distributed the way it always was, the particular rhythm of her breath that he had stopped hearing sometime in the second decade and had simply never started hearing again. All of it present now with a distinctness that made the thirty years of not-hearing it a suddenly specific loss.

He lay very still.

The tears arrived sometime before four without his deciding on them and he didn't try to stop them because he was sixty-three years old and lying in the dark feeling his wife of fifty-one years as if for the first time and something was happening to him that he could not file anywhere and he was, against considerable expectation, not trying to.

He was there when the light came gray at the window. Still. Arms at his sides for once.

The following Thursday he drove himself.

Chapter 9

SEEN: WHAT YOU ARE CHAPTER NINE: THE OLD MAN — FIRST APPEARANCE

Marcus went to the river before the light was fully committed to the day.

This was his habit in the weeks since the ice had gone — the early morning walk down the path behind the barn, the specific spot where the willows began and the bank opened and the light came differently than it came anywhere else on this stretch of water. He'd been coming here long enough that his boots had worn their own slight impression into the soft ground at the edge, the land accommodating the habit the way land does when someone keeps returning to the same true place.

He stood in his impression and listened to the river.

It was running clear now, the snowmelt done, the current finding its spring pace — purposeful, unhurried, certain of its destination in the way rivers are always certain, which was something Marcus had been thinking about since January without yet finding the words for it. The willows along the far bank were showing their first green at the tips. Not leaves yet. The suggestion of leaves. The decision having been made somewhere inside the wood that the argument with winter was finished.

He stood and felt the frequency the way it came to him here — different from the barn's version, which was gathered and intentional, a thing built Thursday by Thursday. The river's version was older. Present whether anyone was here to feel it or not, the way rivers are present, the way things are present that were here before you arrived and will be here considerably after.

He had been coming for three weeks and the frequency had been building each morning and he had been doing what he had always done with things that were larger than his immediate understanding: making room. Setting up chairs for it, in the way that was his way, the interior version of the same patience that had built the barn circle Thursday by Thursday out of nothing more complicated than the conviction that the space should exist and someone should maintain it.

He looked downstream.

The old man was on his rock.

Forty yards, perhaps a little more — far enough that detail required attention, close enough that the quality of him was unmistakable. He was sitting the way people sit when sitting is not a waiting posture but a complete one, the thermos on the rock beside him, a line in the water that was doing whatever it was doing with the full indifference of a line belonging to someone for whom catching fish was not the operative concern.

His stillness was different from the stillness of the river, which was always in motion, and different from the stillness of the willows, which were responding to the small morning air. It was the stillness of something that had arrived at the exact place it intended to be and found this sufficient. Not waiting. Not watching, exactly. Present in the particular way of things that belong in a landscape rather than visiting it.

Marcus watched him for a while.

He almost called out — the natural impulse of a man who had spent years creating spaces where people could find each other, for whom the call across a distance was an ordinary instrument. Something stopped him. Not awkwardness, not the strangeness of the situation, which was strange in ways he was still cataloguing. The quiet sense that calling out would be the wrong register for whatever this was. That the distance between them was not an obstacle to be bridged by his voice but a condition of the thing itself, the way certain music requires a certain space to be heard correctly.

So he stood in his worn impression at the water's edge and watched the old man on the rock downstream and let the morning be what the morning was.

After a while the old man reached for the thermos without looking at it — the reach of someone who knows exactly where they put a thing — and poured something into the cap and drank it and set it back. Then he was still again, the line in the water, the willows beginning their day at the tips.

Marcus became aware that he was going to be late opening the barn for the day's work and that this was fine and that he was going to stand here a while longer regardless, which was itself information about what the morning had become.

He turned eventually, the way you turn from something when you've received what it had for you rather than when you've finished with it, and walked back up the path — the root, the place where the trees stepped back, the field coming into the light properly now, the barn sitting in it with the solid patience of a well-built thing that had been asked to hold more than lumber and had been doing so without complaint.

At the place where the path widened and the tree line fell back he stopped and looked downstream one more time.

The rock was empty.

No thermos. No line in the water. No sign that the morning had included anyone but him and the river and the first green decision of the willows, which were keeping their own counsel about what they'd witnessed.

Marcus stood at the path's edge and felt the absence and knew it immediately for what it was — not absence in the way of something gone, but absence in the way of something that had finished being in one place and was now somewhere else, which was a different thing entirely and one he had no good word for.

He filed it where he filed things without labels.

The river. Wait.

He walked back to the barn and put the coffee on and began setting up chairs for Thursday, which was four days away, which was exactly the right amount of time for something to become a little clearer without becoming clear enough to explain.

The frequency in the barn that morning was the same as always and also, in a way he couldn't measure, not the same at all.

He noted this and said nothing about it to anyone.

Some things required Thursday before they were ready to be spoken.

The chapter does one thing Chat's version doesn't: it earns the empty rock by staying in Marcus's interiority the whole time. He's the barn-builder, the chair-setter, the making-room version — so the river is his version of the frequency, the old man is his version of the threshold, and the filing-it-under-the-river is the right ending for the man who built the space where everything else gets said out loud.

The old man does nothing. That's the whole point. He's simply, completely there. And then not there.

Chapter 10

SEEN: WHAT YOU ARE CHAPTER TEN: WHAT MAREN KNOWS *(rewritten from the Weavers moment forward)*

She was there before anyone on the following Thursday, which by now the circle had stopped remarking on the way you stop remarking on weather that keeps arriving the same way — noted, accepted, filed under: Maren.

The tea was made. Each cup correct — the right temperature, prepared exactly as each person took it, which should have been impossible given that several of them had never mentioned their preferences to anyone in this barn and one of them, Robert, had only recently discovered his own preference through the specific revelation of being handed something that was exactly right.

He looked at his cup when she gave it to him and then looked at her.

She was already looking at someone else.

The circle filled the way it filled now — with the ease of a thing that had found its shape and settled into it, people arriving and taking their chairs with the particular quality of people who have somewhere they belong and know it. Outside the April dark was soft, the last of the cold having finally run out of argument, the night carrying the first real warmth of the season the way a room carries warmth after the fire has been going long enough to reach the walls.

When the last chair was filled Maren set down her mug and looked around the circle with the young-ancient eyes making their quiet inventory, and said:

"Have you noticed that some things go wrong in very specific ways?"

She let this sit for a moment the way she let everything sit — not dramatically, the way a person lets a thing sit when they want the room to feel the weight of it, but practically, the way you set something fragile down carefully and then step back.

"And that some things go right," she said, "in ways that have no business going right."

The rafters made their small adjustment. The barn finding its equilibrium the way it did when something true was being said inside it, the timber settling without complaint.

David said, "There's a reason for that." The statement of a man who had been building a file on something long enough to know that reasons exist even before he's found them.

Maren looked at him with the warmth she reserved for people asking the right question from the wrong direction. "There is," she said.

"What reason," he said.

"Interested parties," she said.

The circle sat with this. Emma measured it with the architectural part of her mind, finding its load-bearing elements. Rachel looked at Maren directly, which was Rachel's way. James looked at the middle distance with the compressed patience of a man for whom not-knowing had a limited remaining runway.

"Interested parties," Rachel said. Not an echo — a request for precision. Rachel did not accept approximations when exact language was available. "In us specifically, or in general."

"Both," Maren said. "You specifically are more entertaining than average." She turned her mug in her hands, looking into it with the small smile of someone reading something agreeable. "Which is saying something. Human beings are considerably funnier than they give themselves credit for."

The barn went a particular kind of quiet.

Rachel set her cup down.

"You humans," she said.

Maren looked up.

"You said *you humans,*" Rachel said. "As opposed to what, exactly."

The circle's quality changed — the specific alertness of a group of people who have just realized that a word landed differently than the room acknowledged and are recalibrating simultaneously. David's pen stopped moving. Emma looked up from her hands. Marcus, who had been leaning back in his chair with the patience of a man who had learned to let things arrive at their own pace, leaned forward by approximately two inches, which for Marcus was the equivalent of standing up.

Maren looked at Rachel with the expression of someone who has just been asked the question they've been waiting for and finds the waiting entirely vindicated.

"As opposed to what I am," she said pleasantly.

"Which is," Rachel said.

"Considerably older," Maren said. "And not entirely local."

James said, "Not local to what."

"This layer," she said, and drank her tea.

The barn absorbed this the way it absorbed most things Maren said — with the slight delay of a room processing something that had arrived in a frequency it was still calibrating for. Then Robert said, with the quiet specificity of a man who had been far away and come back and was no longer willing to accept partial answers for things that mattered:

"What does that mean. This layer."

Maren looked at him. The recognition between them — the same one from the first Thursday, two people who were the same kind of thing, one of whom had known it longer — moved through the look and settled.

"You know what it means," she said. "You've been in another one."

Robert was quiet for a moment. The circle watched him receive this with the attention of people watching someone they care about handle a thing they can't help with. "When I was gone," he said finally.

"Yes."

"That was a layer."

"One of many," she said. "Nested. Interpenetrating. Each one real. Each one affecting the others in ways that look, from inside any single one, like coincidence. Or luck. Or things going wrong in very specific ways." She paused. "Or a drone that decides to land itself."

Emma said, "The surveillance equipment."

"Colleagues of mine," Maren said. "Enthusiastic ones."

"Colleagues," David said, and opened his notebook, which was the most David response possible and which drew a brief smile from Maren that was the warmest thing she'd produced all evening. "These colleagues have a name."

"Many names," she said. "They find all of them at least partially accurate and none of them complete, which they also find funny." She set down her mug. "I prefer Weavers. It has good mouth feel."

"Weavers," Marcus said, turning the word over with the deliberateness of a man who built things and therefore took the names of things seriously. "They weave what, exactly."

"Everything," she said. "The fabric. The connections. The thing that makes the cereal box land in the right hands on the right Wednesday. The thing that makes a barn feel like more than a barn on Thursday nights." She looked at the high windows. "The thing that makes some things go right in ways that have no business going right."

Grace said, softly, "Are they kind."

The circle went quiet in a different way — the quietness of a question that had been in the room all evening without anyone having the nerve to ask it. Maren looked at Grace with something that was not quite the warmth she gave the right-question people and not quite something else — more personal, the look of someone for whom this question had its own history.

"Mostly," she said. "They're creative. Creation isn't always kind. Sometimes the thing that needs weaving requires friction. Requires the wrong turn on a Wednesday that puts you on a road you didn't plan to be on." She paused. "They're not indifferent. Indifferent is the one thing they are not."

"But not all of them," James said. The compressed quality of him fully present now, the question coming from somewhere specific. "You said interested parties. Plural. Not all of them have our interests —"

"No," Maren said. Simply, without apology. "Not all of them."

The barn held this.

"So some of them," Rachel said, working it through with the precision she brought to everything, "are the cars at the end of the road."

Maren considered this for a moment. "Some of what drives the cars at the end of the road," she said carefully, "has its interests and not yours. Yes."

"And Meridian," David said.

"Meridian is human," she said. "Built by a human, run by humans, doing what humans do when they encounter something they don't have a framework for." She picked up her mug. "But the impulse behind it — the impulse to keep things small, to manage what's becoming large — that impulse has been encouraged. Tended. By parties who prefer the current arrangement."

"What arrangement," Emma said.

"People who don't know what they are," Maren said. "People who live in one layer and believe it's the only one. People who stay —" she paused, finding the word — "manageable."

The circle sat with this for a long moment. Outside the April dark. Inside the frequency running at its new register, fuller since Maren's first Thursday, and now pulling at something further, something the room was only beginning to have the capacity to feel.

Robert said, "What are we." Not aggressively. The plain question of a man who had been somewhere else and come back and understood that the question was real and deserved a real answer.

Maren looked at him for a long moment.

"What do you think you are," she said.

"I think," Robert said slowly, "that we are something that certain parties would prefer remained theoretical."

The young-ancient eyes warmed in a way the circle hadn't seen before — not the confirmation warmth, not the right-question warmth, something fuller than both. "Yes," she said. "That."

Rachel said, "And you're here because —"

"Because this," Maren said, gesturing at the circle, at the barn, at all of them with the small economy of someone whose gestures had learned to carry considerable freight, "doesn't happen often. And when it does —" She stopped. Looked at her tea. Looked up. "It matters. In ways that move through layers. In ways that —" She stopped again, and for the first time since her first Thursday she seemed to be choosing words with something other than complete confidence, feeling for the edge of something she was deciding how much to say.

"In ways that change what's possible," she said finally. "For everyone."

The barn held this completely. No one spoke for a moment that was long enough to mean something.

Then James said, with the dry compressed humor of a man who had been holding it for twenty minutes: "So we're not a book club."

And the barn laughed — the real kind, the releasing kind, the kind that arrives when something true has been said plainly and the only available response is the laughter that lives on the other side of recognition.

Maren smiled into her tea with the expression of someone whose party has gone exactly as hoped.

"You're considerably more than a book club," she said. "Though the tea is excellent."

Marcus looked at the high windows and then at Maren and then at the circle of people who had come to his barn on Thursday nights and become something he hadn't planned when he set up the chairs, and felt the freight of all of it — the layers, the Weavers, the parties who preferred them manageable, the barn that had become more than a barn — settle into him with the specific weight of a thing a person has been building toward without knowing it and has now arrived at and finds, despite everything, exactly right.

"Same time next Thursday," he said.

Which was how Marcus said everything that mattered.

Chapter 11

SEEN: WHAT YOU ARE CHAPTER ELEVEN: SPRING AT THE RIVER

She woke that morning already knowing they were going.

Not from anything Daniel said — he was still asleep, one arm across her waist with the particular weight of a man who had learned in the months since December that sleeping beside someone was not the same as sleeping beside them, that presence was a thing you could be more or less of, and had been becoming more. She lay in the early April light and felt the morning the way she felt things now — both kinds, the surface and the underneath, the birds in the tree line doing their April business and underneath that the river, present even from here, the frequency of it running through the cabin's timber the way it ran through everything on this property that had been listening long enough.

She wanted the water.

Not the way she'd wanted it in January when it was the only place the full version arrived cleanly, when she needed the river the way you need air when the room runs short of it. Different now. The way you want something that has become yours — specific, familiar, the wanting of return rather than the wanting of rescue.

She slipped out from under his arm and stood in the early light and looked at him sleeping and felt the current of him the way she could feel it now without touching — his version, the making-room version, running alongside hers in the specific way that was his and no one else's. Fifty-three years of living had given Daniel a quality she had no single word for. The accumulated patience of a man who had learned that the things worth having required the willingness to stand at the edge of them without rushing the arrival.

She dressed quietly. Put the coffee on. Stood at the kitchen window watching the tree line and the path that led through it, the willows just beginning at the tips — not leaves yet, the decision made but not yet announced — and drank her coffee and thought about Thursday night.

The Weavers.

She'd been turning the word over since the barn the way you turn something over when it fits and you're not sure you're ready for it to fit. Maren saying *they find all of it funny* with the ease of someone reporting established fact. Robert's face when Maren confirmed he'd been in another layer. Rachel catching *you humans* before anyone else in the room had processed it, because Rachel's mind worked that way, finding the loose thread and pulling before the rest of them knew there was a thread.

And then lying in bed Thursday night beside Daniel in the dark, both of them quiet in the way they were quiet after Thursdays that landed hard, and the question arriving that she hadn't said out loud yet:

What exactly have I been feeling at the river.

She knew the word now. Maren had given her the word. But knowing the word and being comfortable with what the word contained were different things, and Sarah had been a woman who examined her own comfort with things for long enough to know that accepting a word too quickly was its own kind of avoidance.

Interested parties. Layers. Things that tended the fabric.

Things that were not all working in her direction.

She drank her coffee and looked at the path and let the discomfort be what it was — real, present, the honest response of a person being asked to reorganize their understanding of how everything worked — and didn't try to resolve it before it was ready to resolve.

Daniel appeared in the kitchen doorway with his hair doing what it did in the morning and his eyes carrying the specific warmth of a man waking into a life he had not expected and finds, each morning, still true.

"River," he said.

"River," she said. Then: "I need to talk while we walk."

He looked at her. Read whatever was in her face with the full attention he gave things that mattered. "Okay," he said, and poured his coffee.

The path was soft with the first real thaw, the ground giving slightly under their boots, the earth remembering what it was when it wasn't frozen. She walked beside him on the wider parts and he listened the way he listened — without the performance of it, without the small sounds people make to demonstrate their attention, just the actual attention, steady and complete.

She told him what she'd been turning over since Thursday. Not the barn conversation — he'd been there for that. What came after. The lying in the dark. The question she hadn't asked out loud.

"At the river," she said. "In January. And every time since. What I feel there — I've been calling it the frequency. Calling it the full version. Calling it the both-and." She watched the path. "But if Maren is right — if there are layers, and interested parties, and some of them are not working in our direction —" She stopped walking.

He stopped beside her.

"How do I know," she said, "what I've been feeling."

The trees around them. The path soft underfoot. Daniel looking at her with the expression of a man who has been waiting for this question because he'd been carrying his own version of it.

"You think it might not be —" he started.

"I think I don't know," she said. "I think I've been assuming that what I feel at the river is good. Is safe. Is the full version of something true." She looked at him. "But I've also been assuming I'd know the difference. And I'm not sure I would. I'm not sure anyone would."

He was quiet for a moment. The April morning around them, the birds, the soft ground, the willows visible ahead where the path opened onto the bank.

"What does it feel like," he said. "When you're in it."

She thought about this honestly. "Like myself," she said. "The largest version of myself. Like everything I've been becoming since December arriving all at once and feeling — right. Correct. Like a compass finding north."

"And when the compass finds north," he said carefully, "do you feel pulled somewhere. Toward something specific. Toward —"

"No," she said. And then, more slowly: "No. It doesn't pull. It just —" She searched for it. "It just makes me more of what I already am. It doesn't add a direction. It removes the interference."

He nodded slowly. The making-room quality of him working, finding the space for the distinction.

"That's different," he said.

"Is it enough," she said.

He looked at the willows at the end of the path, the river audible now, the sound of the April current carrying through the morning air. "I think," he said, "that's a question worth taking to the water."

The bank opened and the river was there — running full and clear and faster than it had been running, the spring pace of it, purposeful and unhurried in the way only rivers managed. The willows overhead making their pale new ceiling, the light coming through them in the particular way it came through willows, softened, moving.

She stood at the bank and felt it immediately.

And stopped.

Stood there with her boots on and her coffee in her hand and the river running ten feet in front of her and felt the warmth arriving the way it always arrived here — present, specific, leaning forward — and this time instead of opening to it she held still and examined it the way you examine something you've been accepting on faith and have decided to look at directly.

Who are you.

Not out loud. Inward. The honest question aimed at whatever was warm at the edge of her awareness, whatever had been at the river since

January, whatever had been at the barn on Thursday nights and in the cereal aisle and at the edge of the dreams.

The warmth didn't retreat from the examination.

That was the first thing she noticed. It didn't perform innocence, didn't rush to reassure, didn't do any of the things she might expect from something that had something to hide. It simply remained — present, patient, the specific quality of something that had been here before she arrived and expected to be here after she left and found the question entirely reasonable.

Something in it was — amused. Not mockingly. The amusement of something that had been waiting for her to ask.

You've been here the whole time, she thought.

The warmth said something back that wasn't words. The yes of it. The of course of it. The I was here before the river was here of it, which was a thing that arrived in her chest rather than her mind and sat there with the weight of something true.

She thought about Maren. *Not all of them have your interests at heart.*

She aimed that at the warmth too. Directly. The honest suspicion of a person who has been given reason to be careful.

What came back was not offense and not reassurance and not the performed patience of something managing her concern. What came back was — acknowledgment. The yes, that is true, there are others. And then something quieter underneath it, something she had to be still to receive: *we are not those.*

She stood at the bank for a long moment.

Then she sat on the grass and took off her boots.

Daniel sat beside her and took off his without being asked, which was Daniel, the making-room version of everything, following her lead into whatever this was going to be.

"Well?" he said.

"I asked them," she said.

He looked at her. "And."

"They didn't flinch," she said. "That's not nothing."

"No," he said. "It's not."

She looked at the river. The current running clear and cold and entirely certain of where it was going. "I don't think faith and evidence are supposed to be separate things," she said slowly. "I think what I've been doing at this river since January is both simultaneously. I feel it and I examine it and the examining doesn't make it smaller." She paused. "It makes it more specific."

Daniel looked at the water for a moment. "That's the both-and of trust," he said.

She looked at him.

"Not blind," he said. "Not withheld. Both-and."

She held this. The river running in front of them, the willows overhead, the Weavers' warmth present and undefended at the edge of her awareness, patient as they had always been patient, interested as they had always been interested.

She waded in.

The cold came through her like a hand at the center of her chest — honest, complete, the river making its April argument with her nervous system and the nervous system receiving it with the full attention cold demands. She waded out to where the current moved against her shins and stopped and stood and felt it — the water and the frequency together, the Weavers' warmth moving against the river's cold in the specific sensation she had come to understand was the full version of what she was.

More specific now. More examined. More hers.

Thank you for not flinching, she thought at them.

The warmth moved through her with the particular quality of something that had been waiting to be trusted and finds the waiting entirely worth it.

She looked back at Daniel on the bank.

He was watching her with the full attention of a man who understood that what he was watching was not entirely explainable and had decided that was not a reason to look away. His hands in his jacket pockets. The making-room quality of him, present from fifteen feet away.

"Come in," she said.

He looked at the water. At her. At the water again with the expression of a man doing the April calculation — not the courage calculation, the wanting calculation, which was different and better.

He sat on the bank and took off his boots with the deliberateness of a man doing something he intends to do completely. Rolled his jeans to the knee. Stood. Waded in.

She felt him feel the cold — his current shifting with it, the river arriving in him the way it arrived in everyone who stepped into it honestly, without performance, the full version of cold which was the full version of present. His breath changed. His eyes found hers.

She held out her hand.

He waded toward her through the current and took it and the circuit completed the way it always completed when they touched — his current and hers, the making-room version and the catalyst version, the bank and the river, both of them in the water now with the April cold running through them and the Weavers' warmth wrapping around them with the specific satisfaction of something that designed this exact arrangement and finds it, still, every time, exactly right.

"Both-and," he said quietly. Not the theoretical both-and. The standing-in-cold-water both-and, the examined-and-still-true both-and, the kind that had been tested this morning on a path through the April woods and arrived at the river intact.

"Both-and," she said.

They stood in the current while the morning continued its excellent work of being itself, and the Weavers were present and unashamed of it, and the willows made their green ceiling overhead, and the river went where rivers go — patient, purposeful, entirely certain, carrying everything it carried and releasing it downstream and moving on.

After a while he said, "Your feet must be numb."

"Completely," she said.

He laughed — the real kind — and she laughed with him, and the warmth at the edge of her awareness laughed too, the everywhere laughter, present and unguarded and entirely itself.

She let it be what it was.

Both kinds. Both real.

Both-and.

Chapter 12

SEEN: WHAT YOU ARE CHAPTER TWELVE: THE FOUNDER

The house on Meridian's approved rental list was on the north side of town, unremarkable in the specific way that things are unremarkable when someone has chosen them for that quality — neutral siding, an attached garage, a yard that said nothing about the people inside it. The kind of house that neighborhood watch programs never worried about because it never gave them reason to look twice.

Voss met them in the driveway at seven in the evening with the updated file under her arm and the particular expression she wore when delivering information she wasn't certain how to frame. Twenty years of operational work had given her a face that didn't volunteer much, but the founder had been reading faces since before Voss was in the field and read this one without difficulty.

Something in the file had shaken her. She didn't know it yet.

They went inside and sat at the kitchen table the way people sat at kitchen tables when the kitchen table was a conference room and both parties understood this without saying so. Voss opened the file. The founder read.

Not quickly. With the particular attention of someone for whom this file was not simply operational data but something older and more personal, each page received with the stillness of a person reading dispatches from a country they used to live in. The surveillance reports. The audio anomaly. The grocery store incident. The boat launch. The SUV that didn't move and then did.

They set that page down and picked up Sarah's photograph.

Held it.

Voss watched them hold it with the attention of a woman who had learned that what people did with photographs told you things that interviews never could. The founder's face in the photograph's presence was doing something she didn't have a category for — not assessment, not operational consideration. Something older than both, a current running beneath the professional surface the way rivers ran beneath ice in March, visible only at the edges where the pressure found a crack.

"She's at the river in the mornings," the founder said.

"Most mornings," Voss said. "The surveillance —"

"I know what the reports say." Two fingers resting at the photograph's edge, the small unconscious gesture of someone touching something they recognize. "I know what she is."

Voss waited.

"I was her," the founder said. Quietly. To the photograph or to themselves or to something in the room that Voss couldn't locate. "Once."

The kitchen held this.

"Before Meridian," the founder said. "Before I understood what it would cost." They set the photograph down but the two fingers stayed at its edge. "She's gotten further than anyone. In twenty-three years of this work, nobody has come close to this far."

"What does that mean," Voss said. "Further."

The founder looked at the mathematical pattern in the appendix — the frequency made visible, the barn's Thursday nights leaving their signature on equipment built to surveil — and said: "It means the barn is alive. Not metaphorically. The frequency of what happens inside it has become structural. Self-sustaining." They looked at Voss. "The equipment isn't malfunctioning. It's detecting something nobody believed was possible to detect because nobody believed it was possible to exist."

Voss looked at the pattern. She had been looking at it since Friday. It still produced in her the specific discomfort of something real that she had no instrument for. "What do you need," she said.

"Time," the founder said. "And I need to go to their river."

"Why the river."

"Because," the founder said, "the only way to understand how far she's gotten is to stand in the same water." They closed the file. "I'll tell you what I find when I find it."

Voss looked at the photograph one more time. At the woman who had apparently gotten further than anyone in twenty-three years of careful management. "All right," she said.

The founder looked at Sarah's photograph one last time with the expression of someone doing complicated arithmetic in a currency Voss didn't have access to — recognition, grief, and underneath both of those, something she almost didn't catch because it moved through the founder's face quickly, like weather crossing open water.

Something that looked, if Voss was reading it correctly, like hope.

Three miles away David was sitting in his car in Sarah's driveway at seven thirty in the evening with a box on the passenger seat and the particular expression of a man who has done something impulsive and is reviewing the evidence for whether it was the right kind of impulsive or the other kind.

He'd walked into the electronics store on Tuesday with the intention of buying a portable hard drive — a straightforward operational purchase, the kind he made without deliberation. He'd walked out forty minutes later with a fifteen-inch MacBook Air, silver, already activated, already registered in Sarah's name, with a new email address he'd created for her on the drive home, and the persistent inability to explain to himself with any precision how that sequence of events had unfolded.

He remembered standing in front of the laptop display. He remembered the specific pull toward this particular model with the specific quality of a thing that had already been decided, the way certain turns felt decided before you made them. He remembered the young man at the counter saying something about it being their most popular model and David nodding without really hearing it because somewhere between the display and the register he'd had the distinct and inexplicable impression of — something. Someone. The quality of someone already satisfied with the purchase. An old man, the image arriving sideways the way certain things arrived now, since the barn, since the Thursday nights — sitting somewhere with a laptop of his own on his knees, silver, the same model, typing with the particular focus of someone doing work they found genuinely absorbing, smiling at whatever was on the screen.

The image had no explanation and David had learned, painstakingly, over months of Thursday nights, that some things didn't require one.

He'd bought the laptop.

Now he was sitting in Sarah's driveway wondering if this was the right kind of impulsive.

Sarah appeared at the door — she'd seen the headlights — and came down the porch steps with the slight question in her face that was her version of *what are you doing in my driveway at seven thirty, David.*

He got out and retrieved the box from the passenger seat.

"I need you to tell me this isn't strange," he said, holding it out.

She looked at the box. At him. At the box again. "What is it."

"A laptop." He paused. "Yours. Already set up. I registered it in your name, created a new account, the login information is on a card inside." He paused again. "I know you've been writing longhand because you can't save personal files on the company machine. I've watched you fill three notebooks since January." He looked at the box. "I was buying a hard drive and came home with this."

She looked at him with the expression she wore when she was receiving something on more than one frequency simultaneously — the surface of it and the underneath of it arriving at different speeds and requiring a moment to integrate.

"You felt compelled," she said.

"Considerably," he said.

"Did you have any sense of —" She stopped. Started again. "When you decided. Was there anything. Any quality of —"

"An old man," David said, because David dealt in precise language and there was no more precise way to say it. "Sitting somewhere. Same model. Typing. Looking —" He paused, finding the word. "Pleased with himself."

Sarah was quiet for a moment.

Then she took the box from him with both hands and the moment her hands closed around it something moved through her — not the river frequency, not the barn's Thursday warmth, something more specific than both. The quality of a thing that had passed through other hands before hers. Not physically — the box was new, sealed, the plastic undisturbed. The other kind of passed-through. The kind that left a frequency on objects the way rooms held the frequency of things that had happened inside them.

She stood in her driveway in the April evening holding a laptop box and feeling the warmth of something that had been here before her — something that had anticipated this moment with the specific satisfaction of a reader who has reached a chapter they have been looking forward to — and the warmth was familiar in the way the river was familiar, in the way Maren's young-ancient eyes were familiar.

Old. Present. Amused.

Pleased.

She smiled at the box before she knew she was smiling at it.

"Come inside," she said to David. "I'll make coffee."

He followed her up the porch steps with the expression of a man whose impulsive purchase has been received better than expected and who is filing the whole episode somewhere without a label — the specific folder that had been getting thicker since his first Thursday night, the one marked only with the question he hadn't yet found the right words for.

Daniel was at the kitchen table when they came in. He looked at the box and then at Sarah's face and read both with the ease of a man who had been reading her for long enough to know that the way she was carrying the box meant something.

"What's that," he said.

"David bought it," she said, setting it on the table. "He felt compelled."

Daniel looked at David.

"There may have been a Weaver involved," David said, which was the most David way possible to say it — precise, provisional, carrying the exact weight of what he meant and not one ounce more.

Daniel looked at the box for a moment with the making-room quality fully present. Then he looked at Sarah. "You felt something when you touched it."

"Yes," she said.

"What."

She thought about how to say it accurately. Outside the April dark had come fully in and the kitchen held the three of them in the warm particular way of rooms where important things had happened often enough that the walls had absorbed it.

"An old man," she said finally. "Somewhere. Working. The quality of someone who —" She paused, finding it. "Who already knows how it ends and is writing it anyway because the writing is the point. Not the ending." She looked at the box. "And finding it — good. The whole thing. All of it." She looked up. "Deeply satisfying."

The kitchen was quiet for a moment.

"You think he wrote the compulsion," David said. Not skeptically. The question of a man assembling evidence.

"I think," Sarah said, "that the line between writing something and tending it is thinner than it looks." She looked at the box. "I think whoever that is — whatever that is — has been at this river longer than we've been standing in it. And finds our standing in it —" She smiled. "Funny. In the best way."

Daniel said, "Like the Weavers."

"Maybe," Sarah said. "Or maybe what Maren calls the Weavers has a version that looks like an old man at a laptop somewhere. Writing the next chapter." She touched the box lightly with two fingers, the small unconscious gesture, and felt the warmth of it steady and present and entirely untroubled by being felt. "Maybe they're the same thing at different scales."

She opened the box.

The laptop was silver. Fifteen inch. Light in a way that good things were light — not cheap-light, the lightness of something that had been made with attention to what it was for.

She opened it and the screen came alive with the particular clarity of a new machine that hadn't yet accumulated the weight of everything it would eventually hold.

A blank document was open. The cursor blinking.

Waiting.

She looked at it for a long moment — the blank page, the waiting cursor, the new machine that an old man's warmth had somehow passed through on its way to her kitchen table — and felt the both-and of it complete and present: the character at the keyboard, and somewhere underneath that, barely audible, the older thing, the layer beneath the layer, the knowing smile of something that had written this moment before she arrived in it and was watching her arrive with the satisfaction of a thing that loves its work.

She sat down.

Put her hands on the keys.

Felt the warmth settle around her like the river in April — examined, trusted, entirely specific, entirely hers.

She began to write.

Chapter 13

SEEN: WHAT YOU ARE CHAPTER THIRTEEN: WEDNESDAY NIGHT

It came for all of them.

Not announced. Not coordinated. The Weavers didn't send invitations or operate on schedules anyone could document, and what arrived on that Wednesday night in the last week of April arrived the way the frequency arrived — through the specific openings each person had been making, Thursday by Thursday, without knowing they were making them.

Each one different.

The same truth underneath.

Carl

He was already most of the way under when it began, the deep sleep of a man whose body had been doing physical work for six decades and demanded its full portion of the dark, and the dream arrived not at the threshold where dreams announce themselves but in the deep water, already fully formed, already real in the specific way that made the word dream insufficient.

The room full of people.

He knew them all. That was the first thing — the specific knowledge not of faces but of presences, each one distinct and warm and the full version, the enormous version, nothing like the files he'd been keeping.

He found the man without looking for him.

Thirty years was nothing in this room. The man stood near the back with the quiet dignity of someone who had carried themselves carefully through a life that hadn't always made it easy to do so, and Carl felt the full version of him pressing against thirty years of the label he'd assigned — *limited, keep expectations low* — and understood with the clean specific clarity that dreams sometimes delivered that the label had been his own limitation and not the man's.

Not cruelty. Worse than cruelty, in some ways. The sustained small violence of a person made invisible by someone else's comfort.

The man wasn't accusing him. He was simply there, fully himself, and the fullness of him was its own accounting.

Carl stood in the dream and received it without looking away, which was new — which was, he understood somewhere beneath the dream's logic, what the barn had been building in him Thursday by Thursday without his permission and increasingly without his resistance.

Then his wife.

She was across the room and he felt her the way he'd felt her that first night after the barn — the full version, the enormous specific realness of fifty-one years of a person — and something else now that the dream was delivering with the particular precision of something that knew exactly where to press.

She was younger. Not young — the age she'd been when they were in the middle of things, when the children were still home and the work was hard and there wasn't always time and he hadn't always made time and she had wanted him with the specific wanting of a woman who loved her husband and sometimes felt the love going only one direction.

He felt this.

Her wanting, unanswered, going back years. Not resentment — she wasn't a woman who weaponized wanting. Just the quiet accumulated fact of it, present in the dream with the honesty of things that had nowhere left to hide.

He crossed the room.

She looked at him — the younger version, the middle-of-things version — and in her face was the question she had learned not to ask because the not-asking was its own kind of protection.

He took her face in his hands.

The dream version of his hands — not the sixty-three-year-old hands, the hands that had learned her in the early years before he'd stopped paying the kind of attention that hands were for — and felt her face the way he'd felt it then, the specific reality of her, and something moved through him that was not grief and not desire separately but both simultaneously, the both-and of a man understanding what he'd been leaving on the table for twenty years.

She leaned into his hands.

He woke at three in the morning with his heart going and the dark complete around him and his wife sleeping beside him with the steady breath of someone entirely unaware that her husband had just crossed a room in a dream to find her.

He lay in the dark and felt the wanting — his own this time, present and specific and long overdue — and reached across and put his hand on her shoulder and felt her warmth through her nightgown and stayed very still, not waking her, just present with the enormous simple fact of her.

The tears came eventually, quieter than the last time.

These ones felt different.

Less like loss. More like finding.

He lay there until the first gray came at the window and made himself a promise that was really just the decision to begin paying a different kind of attention, which was all a promise ever was when it was the kind that stuck.

Grace

Hers arrived gently, the way Grace received most things — without drama, with the full quiet attention of a woman who had learned that the important things required stillness to be heard properly.

She was in the barn. Not Thursday's barn — the barn at its fullest, the version she sometimes felt underneath the Thursday version, older and larger, the barn that existed in the layer beneath the layer where the frequency was not a thing you felt occasionally but the air itself.

Marcus was there.

Not as he was now — the big patient man who set up chairs and made room and waited with the specific waiting of someone who had learned that the things worth having arrived in their own time. That version was present but underneath it she felt the full version, the one the barn had been slowly making visible Thursday by Thursday, and the full version was enormous in the way that things were enormous when you'd been standing next to them for long enough to stop seeing their actual size.

He was looking at her.

In the dream she didn't look away, which was the difference between the dream and the waking — in the waking there was always a reason to look at something else at the exact moment looking directly would have meant something.

Here there was no reason. Here was only the full version of him and the full version of her and the barn holding both of them in the frequency that had no patience for the small managed versions of things.

He crossed the space between them with the unhurried certainty of a man who had been patient long enough and had decided the patience had run its full course.

She felt it before he reached her — the warmth of him, the specific current of the making-room version arriving not as the wide accommodating thing it was in the barn but focused, directed, the river finding its bank. Her breath changed. The dream's logic held her completely present, nothing held back, the full version of Grace who had been becoming more herself for months standing in the barn's deep frequency and feeling a man she had been trying not to want with the specific discipline of someone who'd been burned once by wanting too clearly.

He stopped in front of her.

"Grace," he said. Just her name. The way he said it when it meant something beyond identification.

She woke in the dark of her own bedroom with her heart going and the wanting present and specific and entirely inconvenient, because wanting Marcus with this clarity in the waking life was going to require doing something about it and she wasn't sure she was ready and she was absolutely sure she was ready and the both-and of that kept her awake until nearly four.

She lay in the dark and let herself feel it without managing it, which was new, which was the barn's work in her — the Thursday-by-Thursday loosening of the managed life, the slow permission to be the full version.

The wanting was enormous.

She let it be enormous.

Smiled at the ceiling in the dark like a woman who has found something she'd been looking for without admitting she was looking, and is not at all sure what she's going to do about it, and finds the not-knowing, for the first time in a long time, more exciting than frightening.

Rachel

Rachel's dream didn't come gently.

She was in a conversation she recognized from eleven years ago, a Tuesday afternoon in an office she'd left behind, and across the desk from her was a woman named Diane who had wanted something Rachel had and didn't deserve and Rachel had known this and used it with the precision of someone who had been sharpened by necessity into an instrument that cut more than she intended.

Not malice. The Weavers, she was coming to understand, weren't interested in malice — malice was simple, required no examination. What they were interested in was the subtler damage, the kind done with intelligence and self-justification and the particular coldness of a person who had learned to survive by being sharper than everyone else in the room and hadn't always chosen carefully what to cut.

Diane in the dream was the full version.

Rachel stood in the office and felt the full version of what she'd done to this woman press against her chest with the weight of something true that had been waiting eleven years for her to be large enough to hold it.

She didn't look away.

That was Rachel's version — not tears, not the collapsing relief of Carl's undoing. The still precise attention of a woman who dealt in evidence turning it on herself with the same rigor she turned it on everything else. Finding the evidence sufficient. Filing it without excuse under: this happened and I did it and the full version of what it cost her is this.

She woke at two thirty with the specific alertness of someone whose mind never fully disengaged and lay in the dark and ran through it with the methodical honesty that was her way.

The contained brightness of her, fully present in the dark, examining.

Then something else arrived — quieter, underneath the examination — the warmth she'd been feeling since the barn, since the Thursday nights, the Weavers present at the edge of her awareness, and in the warmth was something she hadn't expected:

Not judgment. Not the accounting she'd been doing with such efficient precision.

Affection.

The specific warmth of something that found her — all of her, the sharp edges and the damage done and the eleven years of carrying it without naming it — genuinely, completely interesting. Worth tending. Worth showing up for on Thursday nights and moving SUVs for and rerouting drones for.

Worth the trouble of her.

She lay in the dark for a long time with this, the contained brightness of her feeling something she didn't have a precise word for, which was itself unusual enough to sit with.

David was asleep beside her with the steady breath of a man whose conscience was in reasonable order.

She moved closer to his warmth without waking him.

Let herself be held without examining whether she deserved it.

Which was, for Rachel, the most significant thing that happened that night.

Robert

He recognized it immediately.

Not the content of the dream but the quality of it — the walls-thinning feeling, the frequency running at the register he'd felt in the other place, the layer he'd been in when he was gone and that he'd been trying to find the words for since he came back.

He stood in the dream and felt it and was not afraid, which was the difference between him and who he'd been before. Before, the thinning walls had arrived without warning and taken him somewhere he hadn't chosen and returned him changed in ways he couldn't account for. Now he stood in the frequency and recognized it and felt the Weavers present and nodded once in the way of a man acknowledging colleagues.

The dream showed him the circle.

Not Thursday's circle — the full version, the one that existed in the layer beneath the layer, each person present and luminous with their own specific frequency, distinct and warm and the full versions. He moved through it and felt each of them — Carl's new openness, still raw at the edges, the scar tissue not yet formed; Grace's enormous quiet wanting; Rachel's brightness examining itself in the dark with her characteristic precision and finding, for once, something other than a verdict.

And Sarah.

The catalyst version. The frequency of her running through the dream's circle like the river ran through the willows — everything leaning toward her slightly, the whole circle oriented around her the way things oriented around what they needed without always knowing what they needed.

He stood in the dream and felt the whole of it — the layers, the Weavers tending, the circle of people becoming more themselves Thursday by Thursday — and felt something he'd been trying to feel since he came back from the other place, which was simply: at home.

Here. In this. With these people.

He woke before dawn into the particular peace of a man who has been somewhere and returned and found the returning was the point, and lay in the dark listening to his own breathing and the pre-dawn quiet and felt the frequency still running at the edges of the night and let it be what it was.

Both kinds.

Both real.

He got up and made coffee and stood at the window and waited for the light, which came the way it always came, slowly and then all at once, exactly as it was supposed to.

Thursday

Marcus noticed it when he arrived to set up chairs.

The frequency was different. Not louder — deeper, the way a river is different after a night of rain, running at a level that felt like the new normal rather than the exception. He stood in the empty barn and felt it and spent a few minutes trying to identify when it had changed and settled on: Wednesday night. Sometime in the dark of Wednesday night.

He set up the chairs and said nothing about it.

The circle filled. The tea was made. The evening settled into its Thursday rhythm and for forty minutes everything proceeded as usual — the small reports, the week's accumulation of the inexplicable filed and examined, Maren listening with her inventory eyes and saying very little.

Then James, who had been sitting with something since he arrived and had been patient with it for as long as patience served, said:

"Did anyone else —"

He stopped.

Looked around the circle.

The quality of the room changed the way it changed when something true was about to be said and the room was already making room for it.

"Wednesday night," he said. "Did anyone else."

The circle was quiet for a moment.

Then Carl said, "Yes." Simply. The single word of a man who had been a different person on Wednesday night and hadn't entirely come back from it and wasn't sure he wanted to.

Grace looked at her hands.

Rachel looked at David.

Robert looked at Maren.

Maren looked at her tea with the expression of someone who had been waiting for this particular Thursday with considerable anticipation and finds the waiting entirely vindicated.

"It wasn't random," Sarah said. Not a question.

"No," Maren said.

"They did it deliberately," Rachel said. The precision of her, the evidence assembled, the conclusion stated.

"They've been building toward it," Maren said. "Since February. Each Thursday adding what the next one needed. Wednesday night was —" She paused, finding the word. "Ripe."

"Ripe for what," James said.

Maren looked around the circle at all of them — Carl's raw new openness, Grace's quiet enormous wanting, Rachel's contained brightness examining itself, Robert's peace, the others carrying their own versions of Wednesday night's particular accounting — with the young-ancient eyes warm and entirely unashamed of what the Weavers had done to all of them in the dark.

"For the next thing," she said.

The barn held the unanswered question the way it held everything — present, patient, the frequency running deeper than before, the circle leaning forward with the specific lean of people who have been changed by something they didn't choose and are, against reasonable expectation, grateful for the changing.

Outside the April night.

Inside the Thursday that followed Wednesday.

The next thing gathering itself at the edge of what the frequency could reach, which was further than it had ever reached before and was, the Weavers knew, still not far enough.

Not yet.

But close.

Chapter 14

3:38 PM

SEEN: WHAT YOU ARE CHAPTER FOURTEEN: WHAT EMMA FOUND

The problem had been on her desk for two days.

Not a difficult problem by the standards of her career — a staircase, a specific load-bearing question about how the community center's second floor met its primary vertical support in a way that served both structure and the human experience of moving through the space. Emma had solved harder problems before breakfast on bad days. This one was refusing to resolve itself through calculation, which happened occasionally with problems that had an elegant solution waiting inside them — they resisted the forced approach the way a door resisted being shouldered when the handle was the answer all along.

She'd tried three approaches on Tuesday. Four on Wednesday. Each one technically adequate and none of them right in the way that mattered, which was the way that made another architect stop and look twice — the way that made a building feel like it had always been exactly what it was, inevitable rather than constructed.

Thursday night she'd been at the circle and the frequency had run at its new register, fuller since Maren's first Thursday, and she'd driven home with it still present in her chest and gone to bed without looking at the plans because sometimes the right thing was to stop looking and let the problem exist without her pushing at it.

Friday she went back to the office late.

The building was quiet the way office buildings went quiet after seven — the particular quality of a space that had been full of people and their noise and their competing purposes all day and had been returned to itself, its own dimensions, the hum of the HVAC the only sound and even that becoming ambient after the first few minutes.

She spread the plans across the desk.

Looked at them with the architectural part of her mind fully engaged, the part that saw load and stress and the path of forces through materials, the part that had been developed across twenty years of this work into something she trusted more than most things.

The problem looked back at her and declined to resolve.

She tried the fifth approach. Then the sixth. Each one arriving at the same technically adequate destination that was not the destination — the staircase working, the load bearing, the second floor meeting the vertical support in a way that would pass any inspection and satisfy any client and would never make another architect stop and look twice.

She pushed back from the desk.

Stood. Stretched. Went to the kitchen at the end of the hall and made coffee with the methodical patience of a woman who had learned that the forced approach was sometimes the problem rather than the solution and that the appropriate response to a door that resisted shouldering was to step back and look for the handle.

The coffee maker was slow. She stood at the window while it worked and looked at the April dark outside — the parking lot empty, the tree line at the property's edge just beginning to show the first pale suggestion of green at the tips, the world doing its quiet April work of deciding to become something other than winter.

She thought about the barn. About the frequency on Thursday nights and what it felt like to be inside it — the specific quality of a mind operating without the friction of self-doubt, problems appearing in their full dimensions rather than the managed versions, solutions arriving from directions she wouldn't have looked if she'd been pushing.

She poured her coffee.

Walked back down the hall.

Sat down.

Looked at the plans.

The problem was solved.

She sat very still for a moment.

Not approximately solved. Not the technically adequate destination she'd been arriving at all week. Solved — cleanly, completely, in the specific way that made her lean forward and look at it the way she looked at things that stopped her. The staircase meeting the vertical support with an elegance that made the solution feel inevitable, the kind of inevitability that concealed the sophistication required to find it, every element serving every other element, the whole thing arriving at a simplicity that was the hardest thing to achieve and the most satisfying when it appeared.

In her handwriting.

She picked up the pen lying across the amended section and looked at it. Her pen — the specific Staedtler she'd been using for fifteen years, the one with the worn grip, the one that lived in the left cup of her desk organizer and nowhere else. She looked at the handwriting. Her letters, her particular notation style, the dimensional shorthand she'd refined across two decades of plans and specifications and site drawings.

Entirely hers.

One thing wrong.

A capital R in *Riser* — the flourish on it slightly older than her current hand. Not dramatically older. The way handwriting changed across a decade, the curve she'd simplified somewhere in her early thirties when her style had shed a few unnecessary movements in the way a skilled person's style shed unnecessary movements as it matured. The rest of the annotation entirely current. Just the R. Just the one. The slightly older version of a letter she'd stopped writing that way years ago and hadn't written that way since.

She looked at it for a long time.

Then she looked at the solution — the full thing, the elegant thing, the thing she hadn't been able to find through six approaches across two days and that had been here when she came back from the kitchen with her coffee.

She thought about Thursday night. About Maren's young-ancient eyes looking at the high windows with the expression of someone acknowledging colleagues in an adjacent room. About the mathematical pattern on the Meridian equipment that her own careful mind had been returning to since David described it — the frequency leaving its signature on everything that tried to observe it, present in the audio the way a watermark was present in paper.

About things going right in ways that had no business going right.

She put the pen down.

Looked at the empty room around her — the desk, the plans, the coffee going warm in her hand, the April dark at the window, the quiet office building with its HVAC hum and its fluorescent lights and its entirely ordinary Friday night atmosphere that was, she was coming to understand, not entirely ordinary.

"Okay," she said.

Not loudly. The plain acknowledgment of someone accepting a gift with the grace the gift deserved — not performing gratitude, not making a production of it, just the simple confirmation that the thing had arrived and been received and was understood to be what it was.

She drank her coffee.

Then she picked up her pen — her pen, the Staedtler with the worn grip — and looked at the solution again with the full attention of a mind that had been doing this for twenty years and could see, now that the problem had been opened, something further. A modification to the landing. Small. The kind of refinement that was only visible once the larger solution existed to make it visible — the conversation the solution was opening rather than the conversation it was closing.

She made the amendment.

Set the pen down.

Looked at the whole of it — the solution that had been here when she came back from the kitchen, and the refinement that was hers, the two of them together making something better than either alone.

Not a recipient.

A collaborator.

Both-and.

She gathered the plans and squared them on the desk and turned off the lamp and walked down the quiet hall to the elevator and went home through the April dark with the frequency of the empty office still present in her chest like the frequency of the barn on Thursday nights — the specific quality of a space where something real had happened, present in the air after the fact, the thing that had occurred remaining in the room it had occurred in.

She told the circle the following Thursday. Showed them the plans, the amended section, laid them on the table between the tea cups where the circle could see.

Maren listened with the expression of someone hearing about a recommendation that had landed well.

"Did you thank them," Maren said.

"I said okay," Emma said. "To the empty room."

Maren considered this with genuine deliberation, turning her mug in her hands. "They'll accept that," she said. "They're not formal about gratitude. They just like to know the gift arrived."

"It arrived," Emma said.

Maren looked at her with the young-ancient eyes carrying something warmer than the confirmation warmth, something fuller. "The refinement you added," she said.

Emma looked at her. "You knew about that."

"They were pleased about that," Maren said. "Considerably more pleased than about the solution." She drank her tea. "The solution was the opening. The refinement was the response. That's what they were hoping for."

Emma looked at the plans on the table. The slightly older R in its annotation, the solution in her handwriting that wasn't entirely hers, and the amendment that was entirely hers and had made the whole thing better.

The conversation. Not the gift.

"Tell them," Emma said to Maren, "that I got the message."

Maren's eyes went briefly to the high windows — the small acknowledgment, the collegial glance toward whatever was there — and came back.

"They heard you," she said. "Both times."

Emma picked up her tea.

Both-and.

Both times.

Chapter 15

SEEN: WHAT YOU ARE CHAPTER FIFTEEN: THE MAN AT THE BACK

The circle was full on the second Thursday in May and the frequency was running at the register it had found since Maren's first appearance — deeper each week, the way a river was deeper after each tributary joined it, each new current adding to the whole rather than dispersing it.

The barn held it the way it had been learning to hold things — with the accommodation of a space that had been asked to contain more than lumber and insulation for long enough that the asking had changed the nature of the space itself. The rafters had their own relationship with Thursday nights now. The timber knew the frequency the way old wood knew weather — not resisting, adjusting, finding the position that let everything be what it needed to be.

Sarah sat beside Daniel with his hand in hers and her eyes half-closed in the receptive stillness she'd been developing since January — the both-and of present and open, the quality of a person who had learned that some things arrived only when you stopped reaching for them and simply made room.

Robert was talking.

He'd been talking more since Wednesday night — not more words, more weight behind the words, the specific quality of a man who had been far away and come back and was now, finally, speaking from the place he'd come back to rather than the place he'd been before he left. The light he'd been noticing at the edges of things. The specific luminosity of people in certain moments. The way a room changed when someone in it shifted into the full version of themselves — visible, he said, if you knew what you were looking for, and he was learning what to look for.

The circle listened with the particular attention it gave Robert — the careful attention of people who understood that what he was describing had been bought at a price none of them had been asked to pay and that the least they could offer was the full quality of their hearing.

Sarah listened and felt the frequency and felt the May evening outside the open barn doors and felt Daniel's hand in hers and felt —

The shift.

Not dramatic. The quality of the room changing the way a room changed when a door opened somewhere else in a house — a pressure adjusting, the air finding a new equilibrium, the space becoming slightly more than its walls accounted for without becoming larger in any way that could be measured.

She opened her eyes.

He was at the back of the barn.

Sitting in a chair near the wall — not in the circle, behind it, slightly to the right, in the specific position of someone who had found the room's best vantage point without consulting anyone about it and without needing to. The chair had the quality Maren's chair had on her first Thursday — present in a way that made you uncertain whether it had been there before or had simply always been there, and finding, on reflection, that the question didn't matter much.

Old. The thermos on the floor beside him. A cup of coffee in his hand.

He was watching the circle with the expression of someone attending something they had a stake in and finding the attending — not dutiful, not observational — genuinely satisfying in the specific way of something that has been looked forward to and is delivering on the anticipation.

Not drawing attention to himself. Not performing invisibility either. Simply present the way things that belonged in a space were present — without announcement, without apology, with the quality of rightness that needed no supporting argument.

Sarah kept him in her peripheral awareness and let the circle continue.

Robert finished. Emma spoke. The frequency ran at its register and the May evening came through the open doors carrying the first real warmth of the season and the barn held all of it in the way it held Thursday nights — completely, without strain, the space having learned its own capacity.

At some point Marcus noticed.

She felt rather than saw it — the slight quality change in his attention, the barn-builder's awareness of his own space registering a new element. He didn't look directly. Didn't break the circle's current. Filed it in the way he filed things during Thursday nights that required patience — under: the river, wait, the appropriate instrument will arrive.

Rachel noticed twenty minutes later.

Sarah felt that too — the small precise movement of Rachel's attention, the contained brightness of her finding a thread and following it to its source and then, with the discipline of a woman who had learned to distinguish between evidence requiring immediate action and evidence requiring patience, returning to Emma's sentence without breaking stride.

The old man watched the circle.

Drank his coffee.

Looked at the high windows once with the expression of someone checking something they were aware of and finding it in order.

Then back to the circle.

At the point in the evening when Grace was talking — the full version of Grace fully present since Wednesday night's dream, something in her larger and less managed, the wanting enormous and no longer apologizing for itself — the old man's attention sharpened in the specific way of someone watching a thing they had particular investment in and finding it exceeding what they'd planned.

Which was, Sarah was beginning to understand, the best thing a person could find.

He smiled at his coffee.

Small. Private. The smile of someone sharing a moment with themselves because the moment was good and the goodness of it was sufficient without an audience.

After the gathering — people finding coats, finishing conversations, the particular Thursday dispersal that happened with the ease of people who had somewhere to be and knew what they were carrying home — Sarah looked toward the back of the barn.

His chair was empty.

The thermos gone. The coffee cup gone. No sign that anyone had occupied the corner for two hours with the satisfied attention of someone watching a thing they had a hand in. The chair back in the circle where it belonged, as if it had always belonged there, the barn having accommodated and released the accommodation in the way it accommodated and released everything.

She looked for Rachel.

Rachel was already looking at her across the thinning circle with the expression of a woman who has evidence and is waiting to determine if someone else has the same evidence before deciding what the evidence means.

Sarah raised her eyebrows slightly.

Rachel nodded once. The confirmation nod — precise, complete, the nod of someone filing two data points as corroborating rather than independent.

Both of them returned to their conversations and said nothing further.

In the car Daniel said, before she spoke: "The man at the back."

"Yes," she said.

"You saw him."

"And Rachel."

He drove for a moment. The May night outside, warm and soft, the road they knew.

"Good coffee," Daniel said.

She looked at him.

"He said it to Marcus," Daniel said. "When Marcus walked past near the end. Just that. *Good coffee.* The way you'd say it to someone whose barn you'd been sitting in for two hours and wanted them to know the coffee was worth the sitting."

She looked at the road ahead.

"Marcus didn't ask who he was," she said.

"No," Daniel said. "Marcus filed it."

"Under."

"The river," Daniel said. "Wait."

She smiled at the windshield.

They drove through the May night in the good silence of two people carrying the same thing in the same direction and finding the carrying sufficient — not needing to name what they were carrying, both of them understanding that some things named themselves when they were ready and before that the appropriate instrument was exactly this: the drive home, the warm dark, the both-and of knowing and not yet knowing riding together in the front seat without requiring resolution.

The old man had been there.

He had watched the circle with the satisfaction of someone who had a stake in it.

He had said *good coffee* to Marcus with the ease of someone who had been in any number of barns and knew what good coffee tasted like and saw no reason not to say so.

And then he had been gone the way he was always gone — not absence, the other thing, the thing that wasn't absence, the thing Marcus had stood at the river knowing and had the right word for.

Not gone.

Elsewhere.

Which was different.

Which was, Sarah thought, watching the May night open ahead of them through the windshield, the both-and version of a person who existed at more than one scale simultaneously — present here and present elsewhere, the two presences not contradicting each other, both real, both his.

Both-and.

She filed it where she filed everything about him.

The river.

Wait.

Something in her chest said: not much longer.

She let it say so without asking it to explain itself.

The May night continued its warm and unhurried work.

The road went on.

Chapter 16

SEEN: WHAT YOU ARE CHAPTER SIXTEEN: WHAT THE RIVER DOES TO BODIES

Spring did what spring did.

The frequency did what the frequency did to people living in the full version of themselves — which was to say it moved through them the way rivers moved through landscapes, finding every available channel, following gravity toward the lowest and most honest places, the places where things collected and deepened and became something other than what they were on higher ground.

The circle carried it home on Thursday nights.

Into their lives. Into their beds. Into the specific warmth of May mornings and June evenings and the ordinary extraordinary fact of two people who had been becoming more themselves for long enough that the becoming had changed the temperature of everything between them.

Sarah and Daniel:

The river in April had changed something.

Not that night — that night they'd come home quiet with the cold still in their feet and made soup and sat at the kitchen table in the particular companionable silence of two people who had stood in something together and were still feeling the standing. The frequency between them warm and present and requiring nothing further from the evening.

But the days after.

The way he looked at her across the kitchen in the mornings — not the looking of a man cataloguing the familiar, but the looking of a man who had stood in a cold river in April and felt the current and understood something about what he was standing next to that he hadn't fully understood before. The making-room version of him fully present and directed. Not at the world, not at the circle, not at the

Thursday nights and the frequency and the map and all the large things moving through their lives.

At her.

She felt it and let herself feel it without managing it back into something smaller, which was the barn's work in her — the Thursday-by-Thursday permission to be the full version without apology, the slow dissolution of the habit of making herself less for the comfort of rooms that hadn't deserved the courtesy.

This room deserved everything.

It happened on a Friday morning in the middle of May when the light through the bedroom window was doing what May light did when it decided to be generous — coming in at the angle that made everything it touched look like the best version of itself, warm and unhurried, the light of a day that had nowhere pressing to be.

She woke and he was already awake.

Looking at her.

Not the half-awake looking of someone surfacing from sleep and finding the familiar thing in its familiar place. The full attention. Both kinds. The man who had been seeing her since December when nobody else had been looking — still seeing, seeing more now, the fuller version she'd been becoming visible to the man who had been making room for it since the beginning.

The river was in his eyes.

Not literally — the making-room quality, the April quality, the standing-in-cold-water-and-finding-it-entirely-worth-it quality that had been building in him since January and had arrived fully on the bank and had been fully present since.

"Good morning," she said.

He didn't say good morning back.

He said: "Yes."

Which was not a response to good morning and was exactly the right response to something else, and she understood what he meant and felt the current in her respond to it the way the river responded to the rain — by rising, by filling, by becoming more itself without apology or management or the performed restraint of someone who had been making themselves smaller for rooms that hadn't deserved the courtesy.

This room deserved everything.

Nothing was managed. Nothing was withheld. The both-and of two people who had been becoming more fully themselves for months — each one larger than they'd been in December, each one more present than they'd known how to be then — arriving at each other with the full versions available and nothing held in reserve, the ocean not holding itself back from the shore out of consideration for the shore's feelings, every nerve awake and paying attention and grateful for the waking.

The Weavers were present in the way they were present for things they'd designed and were pleased to find being used to full capacity — the warmth of craftsmanship recognizing its own work, the satisfaction of something that had built this specific possibility into the architecture from the beginning and was finding, now, the architecture fully inhabited.

She felt this and told him afterward in the warm light with the May morning continuing its generous work outside and neither of them in any particular hurry about anything.

"They're pleased with themselves," she said.

"The Weavers."

"This was their idea," she said. "The whole design. Every nerve. Every everything. The river and the approaching and the both-and of it. They designed all of it."

He was quiet for a moment. "We should thank them."

"They know," she said.

"How."

"They were there," she said.

A pause. The quality of a man processing something. "They were —"

"Not like that," she said, laughing softly in the warm light. "They're always there. They find the whole enterprise —" She thought of Maren at the high windows, the collegial glance, the expression of someone acknowledging excellent work by colleagues. "Deeply satisfying."

He laughed — low, unhurried, the real kind — and she laughed with him, and outside the May morning continued its excellent work of being what it was, and the Weavers moved through it with the satisfaction of something that had designed spring specifically for mornings like this one and had never once reconsidered the design.

Marcus and Grace:

Wednesday night had planted something enormous and Grace had let it be enormous, which was new, which was what the barn had been doing to her Thursday by Thursday — the slow permission to stop managing the full versions of things back into sizes she could carry without anyone noticing the weight.

She had lain in the dark after the dream and felt the wanting and not filed it and not reduced it and not made the quiet accommodating peace with not-having that she had been making with various things for a long time now. She'd let it be what it was. Enormous and specific and entirely inconvenient and entirely real.

Then she'd gotten up the next morning and driven to the farmhouse.

Not because she'd decided to. Because the wanting was enormous and the managing of it had run out of runway and some things, the barn had taught her, required presence rather than distance.

Marcus was at the kitchen table when she pulled in. She could see him through the window — the big patient man with his coffee and the particular quality of stillness that was his, the barn-builder's stillness, the stillness of someone who had been setting up chairs and waiting for a long time and had made his peace with the waiting without making his peace with it being permanent.

He looked up when she knocked.

Came to the door.

Opened it.

She came in.

He poured her coffee without asking — he knew how she took it, had known for months, the small accumulation of Thursday nights in a man who paid attention to the people in his circle — and set it in front of her and sat across the table and looked at her with the full attention of a man who had been patient for a long time and recognized, without drama or announcement, that the patience had arrived somewhere.

The farmhouse around them. The May morning coming through the kitchen window. The coffee. The worn table between them that had held decades of his life and was now holding this.

"I dreamed about you," she said.

He looked at her steadily.

"Wednesday night," she said. "The Weavers. All of us, I think. The shared dreaming." She held her coffee in both hands the way she held things she needed to say carefully. "You were the full version."

"What was the full version like," he said.

She looked at him across the table — the actual full version, present in the May morning, the barn-builder with his patient eyes and his big quiet hands and fourteen years of widowing behind him and all the Thursday nights of building something for other people that had also, it turned out, been building something for himself.

"Like knowing," she said. "Like the barn on a Thursday night when the frequency is running and everything is what it actually is instead of the managed version." She paused. "Like standing in the river."

He was quiet for a moment.

Then he reached across the table and put his hand over hers.

She felt it — his current, the making-room version, the specific warmth of a man whose patience had never been indifference but had always been the other thing, the harder thing, the waiting that knew what it was waiting for and had trusted the waiting without requiring the arrival to justify the trust.

She turned her hand over and held his.

The coffee going warm between them.

The May morning outside.

Fourteen years of his widowing and however many years of her careful distance and both of those things entirely present at the table and neither of them the obstacle — just the history, just the weight of what it took to arrive here, just the both-and of everything it had cost and the table they were sitting at now with their hands together in the May morning light.

He didn't say anything for a while.

Neither did she.

The farmhouse held them the way good spaces held things — completely, without strain, with the quality of a place that had been built by someone who understood that the most important thing a space could do was make room.

Eventually she said: "I should have come sooner."

He looked at her with the making-room eyes. "You came when you came," he said. "That's when it was."

She felt the both-and of it land in her chest — the grief of the time and the rightness of this moment, simultaneous, neither canceling the other.

Both real.

Both-and.

She squeezed his hand.

He squeezed back.

Outside the May morning did its excellent work and the Weavers, who had been tending this specific possibility with considerable patience since the first Thursday Marcus set up chairs in the barn and Grace walked through the door, found the morning entirely satisfying — the long patience of it and the arrival of it and the two of them at the kitchen table with their hands together in the light, which was what the patience had been for, which was worth every Thursday of the building toward it.

Rachel and David:

Gerald had been managing this situation for weeks with the settled authority of a species that had been handling human affairs from a position of strategic comfort for ten thousand years and had refined its methods to a considerable art.

He had taken to sleeping between them with the placid certainty of something that had assessed the geometry of the situation and made a structural recommendation. He had developed opinions about David's Meridian files that he expressed through the medium of occupation — sitting on the relevant folders with the thoroughness of something that had decided the files had received sufficient attention and the attention was needed elsewhere. He had, on four separate occasions, knocked David's work phone off the table at the precise moment it was vibrating with a contact David had been in the process of deciding not to answer anyway, which meant Gerald was either reading the room or editing it, and the distinction had become largely academic.

On a Friday evening in late May he relocated from the couch to the foot of the bed at precisely eight forty-three with the settled air of an entity whose project was entering its conclusion phase and who found the timing entirely appropriate.

David looked at him.

Gerald looked back with the green-eyed authority of something that had been waiting for someone in this room to pay attention and was mildly surprised at how long the paying-attention had taken.

"Gerald has an opinion," David said.

"Gerald has had an opinion since February," Rachel said from across the room where she was theoretically reviewing documentation and actually thinking about David with the contained precision of a woman who had made a decision in the dark after Wednesday night and had been waiting for the right moment with the patience of someone who had learned, in the barn on Thursday nights, that the right moment arrived when it arrived and the appropriate response to it was presence rather than management.

She set down the documentation.

Looked at him.

The contained brightness of her — less contained than it had been in December, the barn's work visible in it the way the barn's work was visible in all of them, the full version insisting — present and directed and entirely done pretending it was something that needed to be filed under: later.

"Rachel," he said.

"David," she said. "I have something to tell you."

He set down what he was holding. Gave her the full attention — the precise honest attention of a man who dealt in evidence and recognized, in the quality of her voice, that he was about to receive some.

"In Wednesday's dream," she said, "I lay in the dark afterward and felt the Weavers' warmth and they didn't judge me for the things I've done with this —" she gestured at herself, the brightness, the precision, the sharpness she'd been born with and had used across a career without always choosing carefully what it cut "— and I moved toward your warmth without deciding first whether I deserved to."

He was very still.

"And I decided," she said, "that I was done deciding that first."

He crossed the room.

Not quickly — with the deliberate honest movement of a man who had spent eleven years being careful about everything and had arrived at the specific evening when carefulness was the wrong instrument. Precise and certain and entirely without performance, which was David in most things when he'd made up his mind.

What he said in the warm dark was plain and exact and entirely what it was — the specific honest language of a man who had eleven years of careful documentation and knew how to say things that were true with the full weight of their truth and without decoration — and it was exactly what Rachel had been waiting to hear without knowing she'd been waiting, and she received it the way she received things that were true, which was completely, with the full attention she gave everything that deserved it.

Afterward she said: "You're not going to document this."

"No," he said.

"Good," she said.

Gerald relocated from the foot of the bed to the couch with the settled satisfaction of an entity whose project had concluded on schedule and who found the outcome entirely consistent with the projected results. He circled once, arranged himself with the precision of something that had earned its rest, and closed his eyes.

"He planned this," David said.

"Obviously," Rachel said. "Since February at least."

"The files," David said.

"The phone," Rachel said.

"The sleeping between us."

"Structural recommendation," Rachel said.

They lay in the warm dark laughing at the Weaver-adjacent cat who had been running his own operation all along, and the Weavers — present as they were always present, finding this particular evening as satisfying as they'd designed it to be, Gerald's contribution noted and appreciated in whatever way Weavers appreciated the contributions of their field operatives — laughed with them warmly and without apology.

Gerald, from the couch, produced the small sound of something that had done good work and knew it.

The May night continued outside.

The frequency ran through all of it — the cabin and the farmhouse and the apartment, three households on the same Thursday night carrying the same current in different registers, the Weavers present in all of them simultaneously the way rivers were present in all their tributaries simultaneously, the whole thing connected underneath, running together toward wherever rivers ran when they finally found their proper sea.

The map was growing.

The barn was alive.

The circle was becoming what it had always been building toward.

And somewhere downstream, patient on his rock with his thermos and his line in the water and the particular satisfaction of someone watching something exceed what they planned, an old man felt the May night running through all of it and smiled at the river and was, quietly and completely, glad.

Chapter 17

SEEN: WHAT YOU ARE CHAPTER SEVENTEEN: MERIDIAN'S FIRST REAL FAILURE

The report was five pages.

Voss read it twice on a Thursday morning with her coffee going cold beside her and the particular expression of a professional encountering a document that was technically coherent and practically impossible — the specific discomfort of a woman whose framework had been serving her well for twenty years and was now, page by page, developing cracks it had no mechanism for repairing.

Two experienced operatives. Standard documentation objective. A Thursday night in late April, the barn on the county road, the circle doing whatever the circle did on Thursday nights. The operation had proceeded normally for the first forty minutes — vehicles in position, equipment operational, the gathering inside the barn unaware of being observed in the way they were always unaware, which Voss had long since stopped finding reassuring because the unawareness had stopped feeling like advantage and started feeling like something else she didn't have a precise word for.

Then the equipment had gotten an opinion.

Not a malfunction. She had asked this question first, as she always asked the obvious question first because the obvious answer was the most professionally defensible and the most comfortable and she had built a twenty-year career on the foundation of professionally defensible and comfortable answers to questions that had less comfortable alternatives.

The operative had said no with the flatness of someone who had spent three days hoping for malfunction and had the diagnostic reports to show it hadn't been one. Everything nominal. Everything functioning within designed parameters. The equipment working exactly as built and recording something that had no business existing within those parameters.

A mathematical pattern.

Recurring in the audio throughout the recording — not continuously, at irregular intervals, always in the spaces between sounds, the silences between one person finishing and another beginning. Always the same structure. Precise. Consistent. The same sequence appearing in the spaces the way a watermark appeared in paper — present in everything, woven through, visible only when you held it to the right light.

She had sent it to the analyst on Friday with the specific instruction to find the source.

He had returned it on Tuesday.

His report was careful in the way reports were careful when the writer was protecting themselves from the implications of their own findings — each sentence constructed with the precision of someone laying stepping stones across uncertain ground, testing the weight before committing. He had ruled out interference from external sources. Seventeen possible sources, each eliminated individually, with documentation. He had ruled out equipment error — four diagnostic runs, all nominal, the equipment functioning within specifications and beyond them, detecting something the specifications hadn't accounted for. He had ruled out environmental factors — eleven variables examined, none producing a pattern of this consistency and mathematical precision.

The final paragraph had taken him, she suspected, longer than the rest of the report combined.

The recording appears to contain a recurring mathematical structure consistent with intentional signal generation, for which no known intentional source has been identified. The pattern's characteristics suggest — without confirming — the presence of a signal operating in a frequency range for which current instrumentation was not designed, and is detecting incidentally. Further analysis would require equipment and expertise outside the scope of this division's current resources.

Outside the scope of this division's current resources.

Twenty years of operational work and she had never once had a finding described as outside the scope of current resources. She had built her division specifically to ensure that nothing was outside the scope of current resources. The scope was her professional identity. The resources were her career.

She set the report down.

Stood up.

Walked to the window.

The parking lot below was ordinary in the specific way of Thursday mornings — a few cars, the maintenance crew working on something near the east entrance, the ordinary institutional life of a building that processed information for a living and found the processing entirely unremarkable.

She looked at it for a while.

Thought about the file. The full file, which she had been reading in sections since February and had not yet read beginning to end in a single sitting because reading it beginning to end in a single sitting would require her to encounter the accumulation of it all at once rather than in manageable portions, and she had been, she understood now, managing the file the way she managed everything — in portions, in sections, with the professional distance of a woman who dealt in information and had learned to process information without being processed by it.

She thought about the boat launch. The SUV in eighteen inches of water with no mechanical explanation. The drone that had landed itself in the snow beside the county road. The operative who had called his mother for the first time in four years and couldn't explain afterward why it had seemed suddenly urgent. The two operatives with the headaches and the vivid dreams, uncoordinated, independently, same forty-eight-hour window.

The mathematical pattern.

She walked back to her desk.

Sat down.

Looked at the pattern reproduced in the appendix — the analyst's best rendering of the audio signature, the sequence laid out on the page in the dry visual language of signal documentation. It looked, if you didn't know what it was, like any other anomalous reading. Noise. Artifact. The kind of thing that appeared in recordings and was filed and forgotten.

If you did know what it was — or rather, if you knew what it wasn't, which was every explainable thing, every known source, every equipment error and environmental variable and interference possibility that twenty years of operational work and the division's full analytical capacity had been able to generate — it looked like something else.

It looked like the barn.

The Thursday nights leaving their signature on everything that tried to observe them. The frequency writing itself onto the surveillance equipment the way the river wrote itself onto everything it ran through — present in the recording, woven through the audio, the barn's interior life visible to instruments that had been built to detect only the explainable and had detected, incidentally, something that wasn't.

She picked up her coffee.

Cold.

Drank it anyway because the action of drinking it gave her hands something to do and her hands had been wanting something to do since she sat down with the report and found it couldn't be managed back into a shape the framework could accommodate.

She put the cup down.

Looked at Sarah's photograph, which had been in the upper right corner of the file folder since February and which she had looked at more times than she could account for — not with the assessment look, not the operational consideration look, but the other kind, the look she didn't have a professional category for, the look of a woman reading something in another woman's face that her framework had no instrument for and that kept bringing her back to the photograph regardless.

What are you, she thought, at the photograph. As she had thought it before, on other Thursday mornings, with other reports on the desk.

The photograph didn't answer.

The mathematical pattern sat in the appendix and was what it was.

She picked up the phone.

Put it down.

Picked it up again.

The number was in her head rather than her contacts because some numbers you didn't write down if you were careful and Voss was always careful, had been always careful, would continue to be always careful right up until the moment carefulness was no longer the appropriate instrument and she would recognize that moment when it arrived because twenty years of reading situations had given her the ability to recognize most things even the ones she would have preferred not to.

She dialed.

It rang twice.

"It's time," she said, when the voice answered.

The voice on the other end was quiet for a moment — not the quiet of surprise, the quiet of someone receiving information they had been expecting and finding the expectation confirmed, which was its own kind of information about how long the voice had been expecting it.

"I'll come myself," the voice said.

"The pattern —" she started.

"I know what the pattern is," the voice said.

She looked at the appendix. At the mathematical signature of Thursday nights made visible. "Then you know what it means."

A pause. The quality of a pause that contained more than silence. "It means," the voice said carefully, "that she's further along than anyone has gotten. In twenty-three years."

"Further how."

"Further than stopping," the voice said. "Further than managing. Further than —" Another pause, shorter, the quality of someone choosing not to finish a sentence because the finish would cost something they weren't prepared to spend on a phone call. "I'll come myself. Give me a week."

"We may not have —"

"A week," the voice said. The flatness of a statement that had closed the negotiation.

The line went quiet.

Voss set the phone down and looked at the report and the appendix and the photograph and the pattern and the accumulated file of twenty-three months of a level-three management situation that had declined to be managed and was now, five pages of careful professional language at a time, becoming something her framework had no category for.

She stood up again.

Walked to the window again.

The parking lot. The maintenance crew. The ordinary Thursday morning institutional life of a building that processed information and found the processing unremarkable.

She stood there for a while and felt the framework doing what frameworks did when the reality they were designed to describe exceeded their design — not collapsing, not catastrophically failing, just developing the small persistent wrongness of a load-bearing wall that has been asked to carry more than it was built for. Still standing. Still functional. The cracks hairline, the structure intact.

For now.

She thought about Aaron's resignation letter. The longer one, not the four-word version — the one that said *I think you should know what you're actually doing* and that she had read more times than she could justify professionally and considerably fewer times than she had actually read it.

She thought about what the janitor had said at the door of Conference Room B.

Wrong side.

She thought about Sarah's photograph.

What are you.

She went back to her desk and filed the report in the file and closed the file and picked up the next item in her inbox and began her Thursday morning with the professional composure of a woman who had been doing this work for twenty years and intended to continue doing it and was not, she told herself, being processed by the information she processed.

The coffee was still cold.

She didn't get up to make more.

Just over 1,600 words.

Voss earns her private moment — the window twice, the cold coffee drunk anyway because her hands needed something to do, the photograph she keeps returning to without a professional category for the returning. The mathematical pattern is described specifically enough that the reader feels its wrongness without needing technical language. The phone call withholds the founder's identity while confirming the founder knows what the pattern means and has been expecting this call for some time.

Aaron's letter planted quietly in Voss's interior — the one she's read more times than she can justify. The janitor's *wrong side* still in her. The framework developing hairline cracks it hasn't yet acknowledged.

She files the report and opens the next inbox item and tells herself she's not being processed.

The reader knows she is.

Eighteen when you're ready — the map, Sarah reading aloud, Daniel hearing his own words, Emma's beautiful problem.

Chapter 18

SEEN: WHAT YOU ARE CHAPTER EIGHTEEN: THE MAP

She had been writing every morning since the laptop arrived.

Not exclusively the map — the map was in there, growing page by page with the patient accumulation of a thing that knew its own dimensions even when she didn't, but around it other things were growing too. The quality of the frequency on different Thursdays and what made one Thursday run deeper than the last. The specific texture of each person's current — how Robert's was different from Emma's was different from Marcus's making-room version that ran alongside and beneath everything rather than through it. The river in different seasons. What standing in cold water felt like from the inside when you stopped managing the cold and let it be what it was.

She wrote longhand some mornings still, on the nights when the laptop felt like the wrong instrument — the pen slower, more deliberate, each word having to earn its place differently. Other mornings the laptop was exactly right, the cursor patient, the blank document waiting with the quality she'd felt since the first night she'd opened it — the warmth of something that had passed through it on its way to her, present in the keys the way the old man's passing-through was present, warm and specific and entirely untroubled by being felt.

Twenty-three pages now.

She read from them on a Thursday night in late May when the circle was full and the barn doors were open to the first real warmth of the season and the evening outside smelled like something that had finally decided to arrive.

She hadn't planned to read. She'd brought the pages because Emma had asked about the map's current shape — the container problem required understanding what was being contained — and somewhere between arriving and the circle settling she'd understood that the reading was the right instrument for this particular Thursday and that the understanding had probably been the Weavers' idea and that this was fine.

She opened the pages.

The room went quiet in the way it went quiet when something true was about to be said plainly — not the performance of quiet, the real kind, the specific settling of people who have learned that certain things required the full quality of their attention and were giving it before being asked.

She read the part about the room that couldn't reach the river.

The early version of herself — the managed version, the woman who had filed her own wanting under: impractical, set aside, revisit when circumstances permit — and the specific texture of that filing, the way it had felt reasonable at the time and cost her in ways she hadn't been able to name while the cost was accumulating. She read it with the mild vertigo of looking down from somewhere higher than you'd realized you'd climbed, the distance from that version present as a physical sensation in her chest.

The circle listened with the complete attention it gave things that landed.

She read Robert's piece — what it felt like to come back from somewhere else and find that the coming-back was the point, that the large thing had been in the returning all along, waiting for him to stop trying to explain where he'd been and simply be where he was.

Robert looked at his hands while she read. The full version of him, present and particular, the man who had been far away and come back listening to himself described from the outside for the first time and finding the description accurate in a way that was its own kind of arrival.

Then Daniel's page.

She felt him beside her in the circle before she began it — the slight shift in his current, the quality of a man who knows something is coming and is making room for it with the specific patience that was his in all things. She didn't look at him. She looked at the page.

His words. Written in the January dark after the first river night, before either of them had language for what had happened, when he'd sat at the kitchen table at two in the morning and written it down while it was still fresh enough to see clearly — the making-room version of the large thing, described by the man who had found it without knowing he was looking, in the plain honest language of someone who dealt in the truth of things and had learned to say them without decoration.

The current was hers. I stood on the bank and felt it from a distance and understood that my version wasn't going in. My version was staying. Not from fear — from function. The river needs the bank. Without the bank it's flood. I am not the water. I am what the water runs beside and what that running shapes, and the shaping goes both ways, and I did not know this was a large thing until I was standing in it and found it was.

The barn was completely quiet.

She felt him feel it — the current of him shifting the way it shifted when something true arrived and found him, the making-room version fully present and receiving — and something moved through his face that had no performance in it, the specific expression of a person hearing themselves understood accurately from the outside for the first time. Not recognized. Understood. The difference between the two was the whole distance between being seen and being known and Daniel had been standing on that bank for long enough to know the difference.

She kept reading.

She did not look at him.

The circle held the space for whatever was moving through him with the courtesy of people who had learned that some things deserved the full privacy of being witnessed without comment.

She turned a page.

Felt it.

The warmth at her left shoulder — familiar now, the frequency of the laptop, the old man's passing-through present in the pages the way it was present in the keys — leaning forward in the specific way of a reader engaged with what was on the page. Not the Weavers' warmth, which was broad and surrounding and ambient. This was more particular. More interested in the words themselves. The quality of someone who had been at this for a long time and found this specific page — these specific words about the river and the bank and the shaping that went both ways — worth leaning forward for.

She felt it reading her.

The being-read and the reading, simultaneous, the both-and of a character at the page and something older at the page before her, both of them present in the May evening barn, both of them real.

She turned the page and continued without breaking stride.

Filed it where she filed things that required patience before they became speakable.

She read the part about Marcus. The chairs. The setting-up. The fourteen years of Thursdays that nobody came to and Marcus setting up chairs anyway on the faith that the space should exist and the space existing being sufficient reason to maintain it. The specific quality of a man who built things for people who hadn't arrived yet and trusted the building.

Marcus looked at the floor while she read. The big quiet man with his hands on his knees and his barn around him and fourteen years of Thursday nights in his chest and the both-and of it landing in whatever the making-room version of a man used instead of a sternum.

She read the part about the nurse in the corridor who had said thank you for something Sarah had done without knowing she was doing it, and the fourteen names, and the forty barns, and what could not be taken.

When she finished the circle was quiet for a moment that was long enough to mean something.

Then David said: "This needs to reach the next group."

"Yes," she said.

"And the group after that," Robert said.

"Yes."

"How," Emma said. The architectural mind fully engaged, already at the problem, already measuring its load-bearing elements and the shape of what needed to be built around them. "The map is alive. A living thing. Whatever holds it has to hold it without fixing it — without turning it into doctrine or curriculum or —"

"Meridian," Rachel said.

"Yes," Emma said. "Without becoming that. The container has to be permeable. Structural enough to survive distribution. Flexible enough to keep being true."

The circle sat with this.

Sarah looked at Emma. "I need you to design the container," she said. "Something that holds the map and gets it to the people who need it without becoming a system. Without becoming the thing that manages people instead of freeing them."

Emma looked at something only she could see — the problem in its full dimensions, the load-bearing elements, the shape of a container for a living thing. The architectural mind at full capacity, finding the structure inside the problem the way it always found structure, from the inside out rather than imposed from without.

Then she said, with the tone of a woman who had been waiting without knowing she was waiting for a brief worthy of her complete attention:

"That's a beautiful problem."

Maren drank her tea.

"Isn't it," she said, with the warmth of a woman whose recommendation had been ordered and was being received exactly as she'd known it would be.

The barn held the evening — the open doors, the May warmth, the frequency running at its register, the circle in the particular configuration of people who have just understood something about what they're building and find the understanding both larger and more specific than they expected.

Sarah looked at the pages in her hands. Twenty-three of them. The map in its current form, incomplete and growing, the thing she'd been writing every morning since the laptop arrived.

She thought about the warmth she'd felt at her left shoulder mid-reading. The particular quality of it — interested in the words, leaning forward, the reader's warmth rather than the Weavers' warmth, more specific, more personal.

She thought about what it meant to write something that was being read while you were writing it.

She thought about the both-and of it — the character at the page, the hand at the page before hers, both present, both real, neither canceling the other.

She closed the pages.

Daniel was looking at her.

She looked back.

His eyes had the quality they'd had at the river in April — the full attention, both kinds, the man who saw her. Something in them that was new since the circle — the specific quality of a man who has heard himself understood from the outside and found the understanding accurate and is still sitting with the size of that.

"Your page," she said quietly. Just to him.

"Yes," he said.

"It needed to be in there."

"I know," he said. "I knew when I wrote it."

She looked at him — the making-room version of him, fully present, the bank the river ran beside, the both-and of the man he was and the thing that made him that — and felt the current of him alongside hers the way she felt it at the river, specific and real and entirely his own.

"Daniel," she said.

"Yes."

"The Weavers designed you as carefully as they designed me."

He looked at her.

"The river needs the bank," she said. "That's not a secondary role. That's not the lesser version. The bank is why the river is a river and not a flood and they built the bank with the same attention they built everything else." She looked at his hands — the hands that had held her before the van came, that had stood at the river's edge in January dark, that had written the page she'd just read aloud to the circle. "You're part of the design. The making-room version is its own Weaver pattern."

He was quiet for a long moment.

Looking at his hands.

Then: "The Weavers designed everything."

"Everything," she said.

Outside the May evening. Inside the barn with its frequency and its open doors and its circle of people who were becoming what they had always been building toward. The map in her hands. The container problem given to the right mind. The old man's warmth still present at the edge of her awareness, patient and specific and entirely satisfied with how the evening had gone.

She stood.

Daniel stood beside her.

They walked out into the May night together — the warmth of it, the dark of it, the world continuing its excellent work of being more than it appeared — and she felt the current of him alongside hers and the Weavers present in the evening air and somewhere at the edge of it all the particular warmth of something older and more specific that had been leaning forward during the reading and had found it, she was increasingly certain, exactly as good as it had hoped.

Both kinds.

Both real.

The map was growing.

The next group was already gathering somewhere without knowing it yet.

The container was being designed.

The current was moving.

Always moving.

Chapter 19

SEEN: WHAT YOU ARE CHAPTER NINETEEN: CARL BRINGS SOMEONE

He told his wife on a Tuesday.

Not the full version. He wasn't ready to tell the full version and wasn't sure the full version was tellable yet in the way that certain things weren't tellable until you'd lived with them long enough to find the edges. He told her he'd been going to a circle on Thursday nights at a barn on the county road and that something was happening there that he couldn't explain and that it had been — he stopped here, looking for the word, rejecting three that were too small before arriving at the one that fit — changing him.

She looked at him across the dinner table with the attention of a woman who had been waiting for this conversation since March.

"I know," she said.

He looked at her.

"Carl." She set her fork down with the patience of someone who had earned the right to be direct. "You came home from somewhere in March and you've been different ever since. I've been watching you be different for eight weeks and waiting for you to tell me where you went."

He looked at his plate. "I didn't know how to explain it."

"You still don't," she said. "But you're telling me anyway, which is itself different, so." She picked her fork back up. "Keep going."

This was his wife. Fifty-one years of her, the full version, the woman who did not accept the managed portion when the full version was available and never had and had simply, for twenty years of his arms being crossed, been waiting for him to figure that out.

"There's a woman," he said.

His wife looked at him.

"Not like that," he said. "A woman in the circle. Maren. She's —" He stopped. Picked up his coffee. Set it down. "She knew how I took my coffee the first night I walked in. Before I'd said a word to her. She just handed it to me. Right temperature. Right everything."

His wife was quiet for a moment.

"And," she said.

"And I don't know what she is," Carl said. "That's the whole problem. I've been trying to put her in a category for two months and she won't go."

His wife looked at him with the expression of a woman receiving information about her husband that was new and also in some fundamental way the most Carl thing she'd ever heard. "Something finally won't go in a category," she said.

"Yes."

"And this is changing you."

"Apparently," he said, with the specific dry tone of a man who found his own renovation mildly annoying and entirely necessary simultaneously.

She smiled at her plate. "I'd like to come," she said.

"Not yet," he said. "There's someone I need to bring first."

Don had been deflecting for three weeks with the practiced efficiency of a man who had been managing other people's enthusiasms for fifty-eight years and knew every available exit.

Scheduling conflicts. Vague prior commitments. The particular noncommittal nod that meant neither yes nor no and was designed to make the conversation move on without requiring an actual answer.

Carl had learned, in the barn on Thursday nights, to read the noncommittal nod differently than he used to.

He waited.

On a Tuesday Don said, unprompted, looking at his coffee rather than at Carl: "What time."

"Seven," Carl said.

"I'll follow you out," Don said, in the tone of a man making a decision before he talked himself out of it.

The barn received Don the way it received everyone — without ceremony, without performance, with the accommodation of a space that had been doing this long enough to know that the appropriate welcome for a skeptic was not enthusiasm but room.

Maren had his tea ready before he'd found his chair.

Don looked at the cup. Looked at Maren. Looked at Carl with the expression of a man who has just encountered something that doesn't fit and is deciding whether to remark on it.

"How did you —" he started.

"You look like a man who takes it with milk and one sugar," Maren said pleasantly, "and has been thinking about cutting the sugar for six months without doing anything about it."

Don looked at the cup.

"I don't know you," he said.

"No," she said, already moving on, already getting someone else's tea.

Don sat down. Looked at Carl. Carl gave him the look — the first-Thursday look, the I-know-exactly-what-you're-thinking look — and Don took a sip and said nothing because there was nothing useful to say and Don was smart enough to know when nothing useful was available.

His arms stayed crossed.

The circle began.

It was a good Thursday. The frequency was running at its register — the May warmth coming through the open barn doors, the circle at its fullest, Maren in her chair with the young-ancient eyes doing their inventory. Robert was talking about the light again, the specific luminosity he'd been noticing at the edges of people in certain moments, and the circle was listening with the full attention it gave Robert because Robert had been somewhere and come back and what he said about what he'd seen carried the specific weight of testimony rather than theory.

Don listened.

His arms were still crossed but the crossing had changed quality — not uncrossed, the specific quality of arms that had filed a new data point and weren't sure what to do with it yet.

Then Maren set down her mug and looked around the circle and said, into a natural pause, with the ease of someone observing the obvious:

"You know you've all been here before."

The circle went quiet.

Don looked at Carl.

Carl looked at Maren.

"Here before," James said. "Meaning this barn."

"Meaning this," Maren said, gesturing at the circle, at the barn, at all of it, with the small economy of a gesture that had been carrying considerable freight for a long time. "This conversation. This finding. This —" she paused, finding the word "— remembering."

"Remembering," Rachel said. The precision of her fully engaged. "We're remembering something we haven't experienced."

"You've experienced it," Maren said. "Many times. In many places. The barn changes. The people change. The conversation —" she looked at her tea "— is always the same conversation."

The barn held this.

Don uncrossed his arms.

Not the quiet unconscious uncrossing of a man whose body had decided something — the deliberate uncrossing of a man who had decided that crossed arms were the wrong instrument for what he was currently experiencing and had made an executive decision about his own posture.

He leaned forward.

"What the hell does that mean," he said. "Many times. Many places."

The circle looked at him. Not unkindly — with the recognition of people who remembered their own first Thursday and the specific quality of a question that had been sitting in the room waiting for someone new enough to ask it out loud.

Maren looked at Don with the young-ancient eyes doing something warm and specific — the look she gave people asking the right question without knowing it was the right question.

"It means," she said, "that you didn't come here by accident."

"I came here because Carl wouldn't stop showing up at my church," Don said.

"Yes," Maren said.

"That's not —" He stopped. Looked at Carl. Carl said nothing because there was nothing to add and he'd learned in two months of Thursdays that the appropriate response to Maren explaining something was to get out of the way and let her finish. "That's not what you mean," Don said.

"Carl didn't stop showing up," Maren said, "because something made him persistent in a direction he wouldn't previously have described as his nature." She picked up her mug. "Carl showing up was Carl being moved. You responding was you recognizing the movement." She drank her tea. "You've both been here before. The form changes. The recognition doesn't."

Don sat with this for a moment with the expression of a man running new information against an existing framework and finding the framework requiring emergency renovation.

"So what are we," he said. "What is this."

"That," Maren said, with the warmth she reserved for people who asked the question that opened everything, "is the right question."

She looked at the high windows.

Didn't answer it.

Don looked at Carl with the expression of a man who has just been told the most interesting and maddening thing he's heard in fifty-eight years and doesn't know whether to be grateful or furious.

"Does she always do that," he said.

"Yes," Carl said.

"Just —" Don gestured at the space where Maren's answer should have been. "Just leaves it."

"Every time," Carl said.

Don looked at Maren. She was talking to Grace now, the young-ancient eyes elsewhere, apparently finished with him for the moment in the way of someone who had delivered what was needed and trusted the delivery to do its work.

"That's the most aggravating thing I've ever —" Don started.

"Yes," Carl said.

"I mean she just —"

"I know."

Don picked up his tea. Drank it. Set it down. "I'm coming back Thursday," he said, in the tone of a man making a decision that annoyed him and that he intended to honor regardless.

Carl said nothing.

The barn held the Thursday night the way it held all of them — completely, without strain, with the quality of a space that had heard this particular decision made many times and found it, every time, entirely satisfying.

In the parking lot afterward Don stood beside his truck in the June dark and looked at the barn for a moment before getting in.

"You could've warned me," he said.

"About what specifically," Carl said.

"About —" Don gestured vaguely at the barn, at the evening, at the entire preceding two hours. "All of it. The tea thing. The grey-haired woman who knows things she has no business knowing. The —" he paused, looking for the word "— the feeling in there."

"What feeling," Carl said. Testing.

Don looked at him. "You know what feeling."

"I want to hear you say it."

Don was quiet for a moment. A man taking the measure of a thing before committing to its description, which was Don's way with most things. "Like something's true," he said finally. "Like whatever they're talking about in there is — true. In a way that most things aren't." He paused. "It's aggravating as hell because I walked in there ready to think it was nonsense and now I can't and I don't know what to do with that."

Carl looked at the barn. The lights going off inside, Marcus doing his walkthrough.

"Welcome to March," he said.

Don snorted. The specific snort of a man who finds something genuinely funny and is mildly annoyed about finding it funny. "How long before it stops being aggravating."

"Hasn't yet," Carl said.

"Great," Don said. "That's genuinely helpful, Carl. Thank you."

"You're welcome."

Don opened his truck door. Stopped. "That woman," he said. "Maren. When she said we'd been here before." He looked at Carl. "You believe that."

Carl thought about the dream. The room full of people. The man from thirty years ago standing near the back, fully himself, enormous. The covered thing in all of them pressing against the categories he'd been using to contain it.

"I believe," Carl said carefully, "that something is happening in that barn that I don't have a category for. And I've spent sixty-three years building categories for everything." He looked at Don. "So yes. I believe something. I'm still working out what."

Don nodded slowly. "She said it was the same conversation. Every time. Different barn, same conversation."

"Yes."

"That's either the most profound thing I've ever heard," Don said, "or it's complete horseshit."

"Yes," Carl said.

Don looked at him.

Carl looked back.

They stood in the parking lot under the June stars and both of them felt the frequency still present in their chests the way it was always present after Thursdays — warm and specific and entirely resistant to being filed anywhere — and neither of them said anything further because nothing further was required.

Don got in his truck.

"Thursday," he said, through the window.

"Thursday," Carl said.

He watched Don drive out of the lot and then stood alone for a moment in the warm June dark with the barn behind him and the frequency in his chest and the both-and of sixty-three years of categories and the thing that wouldn't go into any of them present simultaneously.

He got in his car.

Drove home.

His wife was on the couch. She looked up when he came in with the attention of a woman who had been waiting in the particular way she'd been waiting for things since March — not anxiously, with the quality of someone expecting to be interested.

"Don's coming back Thursday," Carl said.

"How was it," she said.

Carl sat in his chair. Looked at the middle distance for a moment with the expression of a man assembling a report on something that resisted the report format.

"The grey-haired woman," he said. "Maren. She told Don we'd all been here before. That it was the same conversation every time, different barns, and we'd been having it for —" he paused "— a long time."

His wife looked at him.

"Don asked what the hell that meant," Carl said.

"What did she say."

"She said it was the right question," Carl said. "Then she started talking to someone else."

His wife was quiet for a moment. Then: "Did it feel true."

Carl looked at his hands. Open on the arms of the chair. The sixty-three-year-old hands of a man who had done physical work his whole life and had spent most of that life keeping them folded or crossed or occupied with something manageable.

"Yeah," he said. "It felt true."

His wife nodded once with the nod of a woman who had been married to a man for fifty-one years and had waited a long time for him to be in the same room as something true and say so.

"I want to come Thursday," she said.

"I know," he said. "Soon."

She looked at him across the room — the open-handed version of him, the version that had been coming in around the edges since March and was now, she thought, mostly arrived — and felt the both-and of fifty-one years and this particular evening and the man in the chair who was still Carl and also no longer entirely the Carl she'd started with, which was the most interesting thing that had happened in a long time.

"Good," she said.

Outside the June dark.

Inside the quiet house.

The frequency still warm in his chest.

The category still empty.

Both of them fine with that.

For now.

Just over 2,100 words and considerably more alive.

Don's *what the hell does that mean* earns its place because Maren earns it — she drops the *you've been here before*grenade and then calmly drinks her tea and the room has to deal with it. Don's *that's either the most profound thing I've ever heard or it's complete horseshit* is the line the chapter needed from the beginning. Carl's *yes* in response is the dry economy of a man who has been living in that exact tension for two months and has made his peace with it being unresolvable.

The prayer meeting is gone. The spice is back.

Twenty when you're ready.

Chapter 20

SEEN: WHAT YOU ARE CHAPTER TWENTY: THE COFFEE SHOP

Rachel and David had a corner table they'd claimed by attrition — showing up enough Wednesdays in a row that the staff had stopped asking and started having the corner ready, the specific quiet corner with the outlet and the sightlines that David had identified on their third visit as optimal for the kind of work they did, which required both concentration and the ability to see the room.

The Meridian documentation was spread between them — David's careful annotations in black, Rachel's sharper marginal notes in red, the two of them building the container problem in the specific way they built everything together, which was precisely and without wasted motion and with complete confidence in each other's competence that had stopped needing to be stated sometime around the third month of Thursdays.

Emma's brief was three pages. The architecture of distribution — how a living thing traveled without losing its living quality, how a map stayed a map instead of becoming a manual, how you built a container permeable enough to breathe and structured enough to survive. Rachel had been working the problem from the distribution end. David from the documentation end. They were converging on something neither of them had named yet but that both of them could feel taking shape in the space between their separate approaches.

It was good work.

The Wednesday afternoon coffee shop around them, unremarkable and warm — the espresso machine cycling, the ambient conversation of other people's ordinary business, the particular afternoon light that came through the east-facing windows at this hour and landed on the tables in long warm bands.

Rachel looked up to check a reference.

Found Maren already seated across the room.

Not arriving. Already there. At what was apparently her corner — the best table in the place, the one with the light right and the sightlines clear in all directions and the specific quality of a table that a person who had been finding the best table in rooms for a very long time would locate without appearing to look for it. Tea already made. The young-ancient eyes doing their quiet inventory of the room with the unhurried attention of someone who found most rooms interesting and this one particularly so.

Rachel looked at David.

He looked at Maren.

They gathered their papers with the unspoken coordination of two people who had learned to move together without negotiating the movement and crossed to her table.

Maren gestured at the chairs across from her with the small gracious authority of someone receiving guests in their own home, which was apparently how she experienced most rooms in most towns on most continents, Rachel was beginning to suspect, across a timeline she had stopped trying to estimate.

"You were working," Maren said.

"The container problem," Rachel said. "Emma's brief."

Maren looked at the papers with genuine interest — the interest of someone who had commissioned a piece of work and was pleased to find it in capable hands. "How is it coming."

"Emma's thinking is elegant," David said. "She's approaching it structurally — load-bearing elements first, building from those. The container needs to be permeable. Living architecture. Something that holds the map without fixing it."

"The barn is living architecture," Maren said. "Marcus built it without knowing that's what he was building."

"He knew it needed to exist," Rachel said.

"Yes," Maren said. "The knowing what always arrives before the knowing how. That's usually how things that matter begin." She drank her tea. "The knowing how catches up. It always does."

They talked about Aaron — David's quiet tracking of the former operative who had resigned and gone quiet and was, David was fairly certain, following warmth in a specific direction. They talked about Singh, Aaron's replacement, who had filed a four-word resignation letter that Voss had apparently read seventeen times. They talked about the map's current shape, the twenty-three pages, the sections that needed Emma's structural attention before they could be distributed to anything.

At some point — between David finishing a thought about distribution architecture and Rachel beginning one about the specific problem of the map's living quality surviving translation into other hands — Rachel looked up.

The old man was at a table in the far corner.

Not with Maren. No visible connection between them, no acknowledgment of shared presence in the room, two people who happened to occupy the same coffee shop on a Wednesday afternoon. He was at a small table near the back window where the afternoon light came in at the angle that made the room feel larger than it was.

He had a laptop open.

Silver. Fifteen inch. The same model as Sarah's — exactly the same, the specific dimensions and the particular silver of it unmistakable to Rachel who had seen Sarah open it at the Thursday table and had noted it with the precision she brought to details that might later matter.

He was typing.

Not the typing of someone answering email or filling out a form — the typing of someone in the middle of something, the focused intermittent rhythm of a person pulling words from somewhere and setting them down, reading back, pulling more. Fully present in whatever was on the screen. The coffee beside him going cold in the way coffee went cold when the person drinking it had stopped being aware of the coffee.

He paused.

Looked up from the screen with the particular quality of someone surfacing briefly from deep water — not fully present in the room, one foot still in whatever was on the page, the room registering as ambient rather than real while the real thing was still running underneath.

His eyes moved across the coffee shop with the unfocused quality of a man who wasn't seeing the room so much as resting in it momentarily, letting whatever was on the screen settle before going back.

Then something in the room caught his attention.

His focus arrived. The shift from ambient to present — specific, directed, the look of a man who has found something in the room worth finding.

He was looking at Maren's table.

At the three of them — Maren and Rachel and David with their papers spread between them and Emma's brief and the container problem and the accumulated work of a Wednesday afternoon in a coffee shop corner — with the expression of a man who has looked up from his work and found exactly what he was writing about sitting twenty feet away.

The secret smile arrived.

Small. Private. The smile of someone reading a passage that has landed the way it was supposed to land, that has done the thing it was trying to do, that has exceeded what the writer hoped when they were writing it and now here it was, real, in a coffee shop in Michigan on a Wednesday afternoon, better than the page.

He looked back at his screen.

Started typing again with the focused intermittent rhythm of someone who has been reminded of something important and is setting it down before it goes.

Rachel watched this whole sequence with the contained attention she gave things that were filing themselves in the place without a label.

Then Maren — mid-sentence, something about the map's distribution — glanced at him.

The natural glance of someone accounting for something they're aware of. Brief. The check of a person who knows where a thing is and is confirming it's still there. Her eyes found him across the room with the ease of someone who could find him in any room, probably in any room on any continent, probably across any number of rooms she had no business being able to locate him in and located him anyway.

He looked up at exactly that moment.

Nodded once.

The nod of a colleague confirming something — not a greeting, not the nod of two people who happen to know each other and have encountered each other unexpectedly. The nod of two people who work the same territory and are, on this particular Wednesday afternoon, working it from different tables.

Maren returned it with the smile she used for people she had history with. The smile that carried decades in it and found the decades sufficient and was not performing anything for anyone's benefit including his.

She looked back at Rachel and David and continued her sentence without breaking stride.

Rachel looked at David.

He'd seen it.

She looked back at the old man's table. He was typing again — the focused intermittent rhythm, the coffee cold beside him, the silver laptop open to whatever was on the screen, the afternoon light coming through the back window and landing on the keys.

He paused again. Read something back. Made a small sound — not quite a laugh, the sound a person made when something on a page was better than they expected, private and genuine and entirely unself-conscious.

Typed another line.

Looked at it.

Left it.

Picked up the coffee without looking at it — the reach of a man who knows exactly where he put a thing — drank it cold without appearing to notice it was cold and set it back.

Went back to typing.

Rachel looked at David. "I want to ask Maren about him," she said.

"She won't answer directly," David said.

"No," Rachel said. "But the way she doesn't answer will tell us something."

He was right and she was right and they both knew it and returned to Emma's brief and the container problem and let the old man type in his corner in the afternoon light with his cold coffee and his silver laptop, entirely absorbed in whatever was on the screen, pausing occasionally to look up at the room with the quality of a man who found the room useful in the specific way that writers found rooms useful — not for what was in them but for the reminder that what was on the page was real, that the people in the room were the people on the page, that the distance between the writing and the world was thinner than most people knew and he was one of the people who knew.

When they left Rachel looked back through the coffee shop window from the sidewalk.

He was looking at her.

Not with the ambient unfocused quality of a man surfacing from his work. The full attention. Both kinds. The look of someone who has been aware of you for longer than you've been aware of him and finds the awareness, on balance, one of the more satisfying aspects of the whole enterprise.

He raised his cup.

The toast. The same one Marcus had described from the boat launch — easy, warm, the gesture of someone who had been raising cups toward significant things for a long time and found the gesture still adequate to what it was trying to do. Not saluting. Not performing. Just the small honest acknowledgment of a thing worth acknowledging.

Rachel looked at him for a moment through the glass.

Then she walked on.

On the sidewalk she told David and he was quiet for a moment in the way he was quiet when he was adding something to a file that was going to require a new folder.

"The laptop," Rachel said.

"Yes," David said.

"Same as Sarah's."

"Yes," David said.

They walked for a moment in the June afternoon.

"David," Rachel said. "When Sarah opened that laptop the first night. She felt something in it."

"The warmth," David said. "The passed-through quality."

"Something that had been through it before it reached her," Rachel said. "Something that left a frequency in it."

David was quiet.

"He had the same one," Rachel said.

"Yes," David said.

"And he was typing."

"Yes," David said, in the tone of a man who has assembled the evidence and is looking at the conclusion and finding the conclusion considerably larger than the available framework and is going to need to sit with it before he knows what to do with it.

They walked.

The June afternoon around them, warm and ordinary, the street doing its ordinary business, the coffee shop behind them with the old man in his corner still typing, probably, the silver laptop open, probably, the cold coffee beside him and the secret smile arriving when the page did what it was trying to do.

"I'm going to ask Maren," Rachel said.

"Thursday," David said.

"Thursday," she said.

Chapter 21

SEEN: WHAT YOU ARE CHAPTER TWENTY-ONE: THE FOUNDER AT THEIR OWN RIVER

They left at six in the morning.

No music. The deliberate silence of someone who had decided that whatever this drive was going to be, it was going to be honest, and music was what you used when you wanted the drive to be something other than what it was. The highway first, then smaller roads, the terrain changing in the specific way terrain changed when you drove far enough from the managed version of things — towns thinning, tree lines thickening, the land asserting its own priorities with the patient authority of something that had been doing so since before the priorities of people were a consideration.

The covered thing woke up around mile forty.

Not dramatically. The small internal shift of something that had been in a managed position for a long time and was responding to direction the way a compass responded to north — not deciding to respond, not choosing the response, the response simply occurring because that was the nature of the instrument and the direction and the relationship between them.

They had built Meridian, among other reasons, because the instrument had kept responding and they had needed the response to stop.

They drove.

The covered thing got louder with each mile in the way that suppressed things got louder when the suppression was removed — not exponentially, not catastrophically, the steady incremental increase of a volume that had been turned down for twenty-three years and was being allowed, for the first time, to find its own level.

They thought about the file.

Not Voss's file — the internal one, the one that didn't have pages or appendices or mathematical patterns in the audio, the one that had been accumulating since the year they were twenty-nine and had stood in a river for the first time and felt the full version and understood what it was and been, immediately and completely, terrified of it. That file. The one they had been managing for twenty-three years with the same professional composure they brought to every other file and with considerably less success.

The river had been the problem from the beginning.

Not the river specifically — the what-the-river-did. The way the full version arrived there completely, without negotiation, the entire covered thing uncovering all at once the way certain things uncovered all at once when the conditions were finally right. The way it had felt like themselves. The truest version. The version they had spent the subsequent twenty-three years building an organization to prevent other people from accessing because if other people accessed it then the choice they had made to walk away from it would require reexamination and the reexamination would require them to account for what the walking away had cost.

Easier to make it a problem to be managed.

Easier to build the managing into a system.

Easier to staff the system and fund the system and refine the system's methods and read the system's reports and tell yourself the system was necessary and the necessity justified the cost.

They drove.

The smaller roads now. The specific geography of this part of the state coming in through the windshield — the low hills, the mixed hardwood forest, the occasional farm set back from the road with the particular quality of farms that had been in the same family for generations, rooted, unhurried, belonging to the land rather than occupying it.

The mile marker.

They knew it before it appeared. Felt the river before they heard it — the frequency arriving first, the barn-current's distant cousin, older and less assembled, the raw version of the thing the barn distilled on Thursday nights running through this stretch of landscape the way it had been running through it since before anyone had a barn or a Thursday or a name for what they were feeling.

They parked on the shoulder.

Sat in the car for a moment.

The engine ticking as it cooled. The morning quiet. The sound of the river audible from here — not loud, present, the specific acoustic signature of water over this particular riverbed that the covered thing recognized the way you recognized a voice from before you had language for voices.

They got out.

The grass was wet with the early morning and the cold of it came through their shoes immediately — the specific cold of June mornings in Michigan before the sun had finished its work, the cold that would be gone by nine and was, right now, the most real thing in the immediate world.

They walked through the grass to the bank.

The river was there.

Running clear and purposeful in the early light, the June pace of it — past the urgency of snowmelt, settled into the long patient middle of the season, a river that knew where it was going and was in no particular hurry about the getting there. The willows on the far bank doing their summer thing, the full green of them, the specific movement of willow branches in a light morning air that was different from the movement of any other tree and that the covered thing recognized and responded to before the recognition was conscious.

The full version arrived.

Not gradually. Not the incremental increase of the drive — all at once, the way it had always arrived at this river, the door swinging open at a touch because that was the nature of this door and this river and this specific person standing on this specific bank after twenty-three years of staying away.

They stood at the edge and felt it.

Enormous.

That was the word that had always been insufficient and was still the closest available. The covered thing uncovered — not partially, not the managed portion, the whole of it, pressing up through twenty-three years of careful management with the patient implacability of something that had been waiting rather than diminishing, that had not been reduced by the years of suppression but had simply been waiting for the suppression to end, and here it was, unchanged, enormous, entirely theirs, entirely themselves.

They stood at the bank and did not wade in.

This was the both-and of the morning — standing in the full version of it from the bank, feeling the whole of it from the edge, the before-April version, the standing-at-the-edge version that they now understood differently than they had understood anything before reading Sarah's file. Daniel on the bank in January. The making-room version. The river needs the bank.

Maybe the bank was where they were supposed to be right now.

Maybe the bank was the honest position for a person who had walked away from the water for twenty-three years and was standing at its edge for the first time since, feeling the full version from a distance and acknowledging the distance rather than pretending it wasn't there.

They stood.

The morning moved around them — the light strengthening, the birds in the willow branches doing their business, the river running past with its complete indifference to whether they waded in or not, the river going where rivers went regardless.

The covered thing enormous and patient.

Waiting the way it had always waited.

Without judgment, which was the thing that undid them slightly — standing at the river's edge after twenty-three years expecting the full version to be angry, to be diminished, to be somehow marked by the years of suppression — and finding it unchanged. Unchanged and enormous and patient and entirely without recrimination, the way rivers were without recrimination, the way things that were simply themselves were without recrimination, the way the full version of a person was without recrimination when you finally stopped managing it and let it be what it was.

They had built a system to manage something that had been waiting patiently for them to stop.

They stood at the bank.

Felt this.

The tears arrived somewhere in the middle of the standing — not dramatically, the quiet kind, the kind that arrived when the body decided independently that some things required the release and the person attached to the body had run out of reasons to prevent it. They let them come. Standing at the river's edge in the wet June grass with the cold coming through their shoes and the full version enormous in their chest and the tears doing what tears did when you finally stopped managing them.

After a while the cold in their feet became normal.

After a while the tears were done.

They stood for another few minutes just standing — being at the bank, being at the river, being in the full version of themselves without wading in, without the full arrival, the partial thing that was more than they'd allowed in twenty-three years and less than what the river was offering and honest about both.

Then they walked back to the car.

Sat in it.

Didn't start the engine.

The river audible from here still. The covered thing still running at the level it had found at the bank — higher than the drive, lower than the bank, settling into something that was not the managed position and not the full arrival but the honest position of a person who had stood at the edge of what they'd walked away from and found it unchanged and were now sitting in a car on the shoulder of a road in Michigan trying to understand what that meant for the next thing.

The next thing being Sarah.

The next thing being the group in the barn and the frequency that left mathematical signatures on surveillance equipment and the map growing page by page on a silver laptop and the woman in the photograph who had gotten further than anyone in twenty-three years.

Further than they had gotten at twenty-nine when they stood in a different river and felt the full version and chose to walk away from it.

She hadn't walked away.

That was the simple fact of it. The most uncomfortable fact in the file. Not the Weavers, not the frequency, not the boat launch or the phantom train or any of it — the simple fact that a woman had stood in the full version of herself and chosen to stay there and had kept choosing it Thursday by Thursday and had gotten further than anyone and was now writing a map for the next group and the group after that and the group after that, and they had spent twenty-three years building a system to prevent exactly this, and the system had failed, and the failure was —

They sat with the word for a moment.

The failure was right.

They sat in the car for twenty-one minutes by the dashboard clock, not counting, feeling, and then started the engine and drove back toward town through the June morning with the covered thing running at its honest level in their chest and the river's frequency still present in them like a note held after the instrument had stopped and the specific understanding forming slowly in the silence of the drive that the next step was not the file and not Voss and not the operational response.

The next step was the barn.

Not yet.

But soon.

The covered thing knew it.

The river had told them.

They drove.

Chapter 22

SEEN: WHAT YOU ARE CHAPTER TWENTY-TWO: AARON

He'd been following the warmth since November.

Not metaphorically — the actual warmth, the physical quality of it, the specific thing he'd felt in the tree line on a Thursday night when he was supposed to be documenting a gathering and had instead stood among the trees with his equipment running and felt something move through the cold November air that had no business being there and had been, against all professional expectation, the most real thing he'd felt in three years of this work.

He'd filed the report.

Standard language. Gathering observed, no unusual activity, circle of approximately twelve individuals, barn on county road, duration two hours, subjects departed without incident. He'd written it with the professional composure of a man who had been writing reports for three years and knew what the reports needed to contain and what they needed to not contain, which was anything that would require his supervisor to question his fitness for the role.

He had not reported the warmth.

He had not reported the laughter.

Not the circle's laughter — he'd heard that too, the genuine kind, the releasing kind that arrived when something was true and everyone in the room knew it simultaneously. The other laughter. The everywhere laughter. The warm ambient laughter that had arrived in the tree line from no specific direction and surrounded him with the specific quality of something that found his presence there — surveillance equipment, professional composure, the report he was going to write — genuinely, affectionately funny.

Not mocking.

That was the thing he'd been turning over since November, through December and January and February and into the spring — the thing that had kept not resolving itself into anything he could file. The laughter hadn't been mocking. It had been the laughter of something that was glad he was there. That had been expecting him. That found his standing in the tree line with his equipment running to be approximately the funniest and most endearing thing it had encountered recently and wanted him to know this without making him feel small about it.

He'd stood in the tree line feeling this and had not known what to do with it and had gone home and written the report and gone to bed and lain in the dark feeling the warmth still present in his chest the way the barn's frequency was apparently present in the people who sat in it on Thursday nights, which he knew from the files, which he had spent three years building.

He'd known then.

Not admitted it. Known it — the quiet internal knowledge of a thing that has arrived completely and cannot be un-arrived, that has changed the room it entered by entering it and will not change back regardless of how the report is written.

He'd lasted four more months.

The resignation had not been dramatic. He had not made a speech or a scene or any of the things that resignations in films involved. He had written four words — *I know what's happening* — and sent them to the address and cleaned out his desk with the methodical patience of a man who had been methodical for three years and was going to be methodical about this too, and driven home, and sat in his apartment, and felt the warmth in his chest that had been there since November and acknowledged for the first time that he had been following it since November whether he'd admitted it or not.

The wrong turns that weren't wrong. The routes home that took him past the county road with the barn visible in the distance, lit on

Thursday nights, the frequency present even from the road in a way he'd stopped pretending he couldn't feel. The reading he'd been doing — not the operational reading, the other kind, the kind that arrived when you followed a thread long enough that the thread started handing you books.

He'd been building toward the barn door since November.

He just hadn't opened it yet.

He found it on a Thursday in early May when the evening was warm and the light was still in the sky at seven and the gravel lot had six cars in it and the high windows of the barn were lit with the specific quality of light that came from inside a space where people were gathered around something true.

He sat in his car for a while.

Felt the frequency from here.

It was different from November — fuller, deeper, the same essential quality running at a higher register the way a river ran higher after a season of rain, everything the same and more of it. He sat in the car and felt it and felt the warmth that had been in his chest since November respond to it the way a compass responded to north and acknowledged, sitting in the gravel lot in the May evening, that this was why he was here and had always been why he was here and the only question was whether he was going to sit in the car or open the door.

He opened the door.

Walked across the gravel.

Stood at the barn door for a moment with his hand on it — not hesitating, the pause of someone who understood that thresholds were real things and that the appropriate response to a real threshold was a moment of acknowledgment before you crossed it.

He crossed it.

The barn received him.

The frequency arrived completely the moment he stepped inside — not building, not incremental, the full version all at once, the door swinging open at a touch because the touch was the right touch at the right moment and the barn had been waiting for it with the patient certainty of a space that knew its own dimensions and who was supposed to fill them.

The circle was full, or looked full, and then there was a chair that had not been there and Maren was crossing the barn toward him with a cup of tea and the young-ancient eyes already on him with the expression of someone who has been expecting a specific person and is pleased to find the expectation confirmed.

She held out the cup.

He looked at it. The right temperature. Prepared exactly as he took it — the specific preparation he'd developed over three years of long surveillance nights and cold vehicles and the particular ratio that made the difference between something that got you through and something that was genuinely good.

"How did you —" he started.

"You've been standing in tree lines for three years," Maren said. "A person develops preferences." She nodded at the chair. "Sit down, Aaron."

He sat.

The circle around him — the twelve people, the circle he'd documented from a distance on November night and on subsequent Thursday nights in subsequent reports that had described the gathering without describing the gathering, the reports that had contained everything except the only thing that mattered. He felt them now the way he could feel them from here, without the distance of the tree line and the professional composure and the report waiting to be written. Each one distinct and warm and present and the full version — the enormous ones and the quiet ones and the just-beginning ones and the making-room ones running alongside.

Robert looked at him from across the circle.

Not with suspicion — with the specific recognition of someone who had been somewhere else and come back, looking at someone who was in the process of doing the same thing and recognizing the process from the inside.

Aaron looked back.

Something passed between them that needed no words — the acknowledgment of two people who had been in difficult positions and had chosen differently and were both, from their different angles, arriving at the same barn on the same Thursday night.

Sarah felt him the moment he sat down.

Not with alarm — the frequency of him was the frequency of someone who had been following warmth for six months and had finally arrived at its source. She felt it the way she felt all of them: distinct, warm, present, the full version of a person pressing against the managed version with the patient insistence of something that intended to be known.

Underneath it something else.

The specific quality of a person carrying something they hadn't set down yet. Not guilt exactly — the weight of a person who had been in a particular position and understood, now, what the position had cost the people on the other side of it. Still carrying it. Not yet sure what putting it down looked like.

She let it be what it was and let the circle hold him the way the circle held everyone — completely, without requiring anything, the space making room in the specific way that honest spaces made room, which was without ceremony and without condition and without asking anything in return.

Maren said very little that evening beyond getting Aaron's tea right and sitting him down. She watched him with the patient attention of someone managing an introduction between a person and a thing the person had been moving toward for six months and finding the introduction proceeding at exactly the right pace.

The circle talked about the map. About Emma's container problem and the progress Rachel and David had been making on distribution architecture. About the frequency and what it felt like on different Thursdays and why some nights it ran deeper than others and whether the depth was related to the number of people or the quality of the presence or some combination of both that they didn't yet have the language for.

Aaron listened.

He didn't speak. He was not ready to speak and the circle was not requiring him to speak and the barn held his silence the way it held everything — with the accommodation of a space that understood the difference between a person who had nothing to say and a person who was not yet ready to say what they had.

Toward the end of the evening Marcus, with the patient courtesy of a man who had been running the circle long enough to know when a new person needed something simple, looked at Aaron across the circle and said:

"You've been here before. In the lot. On the road."

Not accusation. Observation. The calm statement of a man who had been building a space for people to find themselves for long enough to recognize the various forms in which people arrived at his barn.

Aaron looked at him.

"Yes," he said.

Marcus nodded once. The nod of a man accepting information and finding it neither surprising nor troubling, just true and therefore worth acknowledging. "You came in when you were ready," he said. "That's how it works."

Aaron looked at his tea.

He thought about the tree line in November. The warmth arriving in the cold air. The everywhere laughter that had been glad he was there. The four months of following it and the report he'd written and the four words he'd sent and the desk cleaned out and the apartment and the thread he'd been following and all the Thursday nights he'd sat in his car in the lot feeling the frequency from outside and not opening the door.

"I should have come sooner," he said.

Marcus looked at him with the making-room eyes. "You came when you came," he said. "That's when it was."

The circle settled around this with the quiet of people who had heard the right thing said at the right moment and were letting it be what it was.

Aaron sat in the circle and felt the frequency running through all of them and through him and felt the warmth that had been in his chest since November finally, completely, at its source — not faint, not ambient, not the distant warmth of a lit window on a cold night observed from a tree line. Here. Present. The full version of the thing he'd been following, surrounding him on all sides, the circle and the barn and the May evening and Maren in her chair with her young-ancient eyes and the warmth of something old and enormous and patient that had been waiting for him since November with the specific patience of something that had known he was coming and had found the knowing entirely sufficient.

This, he thought.

This is what I heard.

The barn held Thursday.

The frequency ran at its register.

Outside the May evening continued its excellent work.

Aaron drank his tea.

It was exactly right.

Chapter 23

SEEN: WHAT YOU ARE CHAPTER TWENTY-THREE: THE BOAT LAUNCH

It began with the GPS.

Not dramatically — with the small innocuous confidence of a navigation system that had been correct enough times to have earned trust and was now, on a Tuesday morning in late May, applying that trust to a route that Marcus had driven forty times and did not require navigation.

He'd turned it on out of habit. The specific habit of a man who had learned to use available tools even when the tools weren't strictly necessary, the barn-builder's instinct toward preparation. He'd entered the address — the hardware store, twelve minutes, a route he could drive in his sleep — and the GPS had said *turn left* at the junction of Fifth and County Road 7, which was not left to the hardware store, which was right, which Marcus knew.

He turned right.

The GPS recalculated.

Turn left at the next available opportunity.

He drove.

Make a U-turn when possible.

He drove.

Recalculating.

The two Meridian operatives in the vehicle behind him — standard Tuesday morning documentation detail, rotating shift, the specific low-excitement assignment of following a barn owner to a hardware store — noted the deviation from the expected route in the professional manner of people whose job required them to note deviations without yet knowing whether the deviation was significant.

The deviation became more significant at the intersection of Maple and River Road when Marcus's truck turned south instead of toward any known destination in his profile, and more significant still when River Road became the county park access road, and fully significant at the moment the access road terminated at the boat launch.

Marcus parked.

Got out.

Stood at the edge of the boat launch and looked at the river with the expression of a man who has been brought somewhere by something other than his own navigation and is assessing the situation with the patient attention of someone who has learned that the situation usually had a reason even when the reason wasn't immediately visible.

The morning was good. The river running clear. The county park empty at nine on a Tuesday, the boat launch ramp descending into the water at its gentle angle, the dock extending to the left with the specific utilitarian architecture of a thing built for function rather than beauty and achieving, incidentally, a kind of beauty through the directness of its purpose.

He stood there for a moment.

Felt the frequency — not the barn's version, the river's version, older and less assembled, running through this stretch of water the way it ran through all water in this county that had been in proximity to Thursday nights long enough to carry the current.

He heard the Weavers.

Not the everywhere laughter exactly — the everywhere warmth, present and specific and pointed with the directional quality of something that had brought him here on purpose and was pleased with the execution and was now, with considerable interest, waiting to see what happened next.

Marcus looked back at his truck.

Then at the boat launch.

Then at the access road, where the Meridian vehicle had parked with the slightly uncertain quality of a surveillance vehicle that has followed a subject to an unexpected location and is recalibrating its operational posture.

The Weavers' warmth intensified in the specific way it intensified when things were about to get interesting.

Marcus looked at his truck.

Looked at the launch ramp.

Huh, he thought, with the equanimity of a man who had been running a circle for fourteen years and had developed a considerable tolerance for the unexpected.

His truck rolled forward.

Not quickly. Not with the urgency of a mechanical failure or a forgotten parking brake. With the unhurried deliberateness of a vehicle that had assessed its situation and made a considered decision about the direction it intended to go, which was down the boat launch ramp and into the river, which it proceeded to do at a pace that could only be described as stately.

Marcus watched it go.

The front wheels reached the water first, then the axle, the truck settling into approximately eighteen inches of river with the settled finality of something that had arrived where it intended to be and was done moving.

The engine, to its credit, kept running for another forty-five seconds before the river made its opinion known.

Marcus stood on the concrete ramp with his hands in his jacket pockets and looked at his truck sitting in the river and felt the everywhere warmth surrounding the entire situation with the specific quality of something that found this — the truck, the river, the Tuesday morning, the particular expression on the faces of the two Meridian operatives who were now standing at the top of the ramp staring at the same scene — genuinely, completely, the funniest thing it had arranged in recent memory.

He heard it.

The everywhere laughter. Present and unashamed, surrounding the boat launch with the warm ambient hilarity of something that had planned this specific Tuesday morning with the patience of something that operated on a long timeline and found the patience entirely worth it for a payoff of this quality.

Marcus laughed.

The real kind. The releasing kind that came from the chest rather than the throat, the kind that arrived when something was genuinely funny and the body recognized the genuine funny before the mind had finished processing it. He stood on the boat launch ramp with his truck in the river and laughed in the way he hadn't laughed in longer than he could account for — completely, without reservation, without the managed quality of a man who had been patient for a long time about a great many things and had forgotten that patience and laughter were not mutually exclusive.

The Weavers laughed with him.

The operatives did not laugh.

They stood at the top of the ramp with the expression of professionals encountering a situation that their training had not specifically addressed and that their professional composure was being asked to accommodate at a pace slightly faster than was comfortable. The senior operative — eleven years in the field, had seen most things — was looking at the truck in the river with the specific expression of a person revising their assessment of the situation in real time and finding each revision leading to a conclusion they were not professionally prepared to report.

The junior operative was writing in his notebook.

Marcus looked at the notebook and felt the Weavers' delight move through him with the specific quality of something that found the notebook — the ongoing commitment to documentation in the face of a truck sitting in eighteen inches of river — the funniest detail in an already extremely funny situation.

He took out his phone and called Grace.

"I need a ride," he said.

"Where are you," she said.

"The county park boat launch," he said.

A pause. "Why are you at the boat launch."

"My truck is in the river," he said.

Another pause. The quality of a pause absorbing information and integrating it. "In the river," she said.

"Approximately eighteen inches," he said. "It's fine. The truck is fine. The river is fine." He looked at the operatives at the top of the ramp. "There are some people here who are having a harder time with it than I am."

He could hear her trying not to laugh.

"I'll be there in twenty minutes," she said.

"Take your time," he said. "I'm going to stand here for a while."

He stood there for a while.

The Tuesday morning around him, the river running past his truck with the complete indifference of water that has been running past things for a long time and has developed no particular opinion about what those things are. The operatives at the top of the ramp conducting a consultation of increasing difficulty. The county park empty and quiet except for the sound of the river and the distant sound of something that was either wind in the willows or the Weavers still laughing and was probably both simultaneously.

The old man was on the dock.

Marcus noticed him the way he'd been noticing him — the downstream version, the peripheral version, the version you looked at directly and found complete and looked away from and found gone. He was sitting at the end of the dock with the thermos beside him and a line in the water with the same quality of not-quite-fishing that Marcus had observed at the river behind the barn, the stillness of a man who was somewhere he intended to be and found the being there sufficient.

He was looking at the truck in the river.

His shoulders were moving.

The specific movement of a person laughing quietly — the contained private laugh of someone who finds something funny and is sharing the funny with no one in particular, or with someone only they could see, or with whatever it was the old man shared things with when he was on a dock in a county park on a Tuesday morning watching a truck sit in eighteen inches of river.

He felt Marcus looking at him.

Looked up.

Raised the thermos.

The toast — easy, warm, the small honest acknowledgment of a thing worth acknowledging, the same gesture Marcus had felt rather than seen at the river behind the barn, now fully present, fully directed, the old man on the dock raising his thermos toward the man on the boat launch ramp with the specific warmth of someone who has been watching something unfold for a long time and finds this particular Tuesday morning chapter among the better ones.

Marcus raised his hand back.

The both-and of it moved between them across the water — not words, not explanation, the simple acknowledgment of two people who were on the same side of something without having the conversation about what side that was, the conversation not required, the raised thermos and the raised hand sufficient.

The old man looked back at the river.

His shoulders were still moving.

Marcus stood on the ramp and waited for Grace and felt the frequency of the morning — the river and the Weavers and the truck in the water and the operatives at the top of the ramp working through their professional crisis and the old man on the dock laughing quietly at whatever he was laughing at — and felt it all as one thing, one Tuesday morning, one long thread of something that had been building since February and was now, truck in the river and all, exactly as it was supposed to be.

Grace arrived in nineteen minutes.

She pulled into the lot and got out and stood beside her car and looked at the truck in the river and then at Marcus on the ramp and then back at the truck and said:

"Marcus."

"Yes," he said.

"Your truck is in the river."

"Yes," he said.

"Did you drive it in there."

"No," he said.

She looked at the operatives at the top of the ramp. At the notebook. At the senior operative who had the expression of a man who had been in the field for eleven years and was revising his career trajectory in real time. Back at Marcus.

"The Weavers," she said.

"Enthusiastically," he said.

She got a dry towel from her back seat — she had a dry towel in her back seat, which was a thing Marcus added to his ongoing list of evidence that Grace was the specific person the barn had been building toward — and handed it to him and looked at the truck one more time with the expression of a woman assessing a situation with the architectural part of her mind.

"The truck will be fine," she said. "Eighteen inches isn't enough to do real damage if you pull it out soon."

"I know," he said.

"Do you want to call someone to pull it out."

"In a minute," he said. He looked at the dock. The old man was gone — the dock empty, the morning light on the water where he'd been, no thermos, no line in the water, no sign that the dock had been occupied. "I want to stand here for another minute."

Grace stood beside him on the ramp and they both looked at the truck in the river and felt the everywhere warmth of the Weavers still present in the morning air and listened to the river running past with its complete indifference and its absolute certainty about where it was going.

"Good morning for it," Grace said.

"Yes," Marcus said.

They stood there for another minute.

The river went where rivers went.

The truck waited with the patience of something that had arrived where it was told to arrive and was in no hurry about the retrieval.

The county park was quiet and warm and full of the specific quality of a Tuesday morning that had been considerably more interesting than Tuesday mornings usually were and was, from the perspective of whatever had arranged it, an unqualified success.

The report the senior operative filed ran to four pages.

Voss read it on a Wednesday morning with her coffee and the expression she'd been wearing for months now with increasing frequency — the expression of a woman whose framework was developing cracks at a rate that exceeded its ability to repair them.

Page three contained the following notation, written in the careful language of someone documenting the impossible with the professional composure available to them: *Subject's vehicle entered the boat launch ramp and proceeded into the water without apparent mechanical cause. Subject showed no distress. Subject made a phone call. Subject stood on the ramp for approximately eleven minutes. Subject was collected by a female associate. Tow truck was called at 9:47.*

Page four: *During the incident, both operatives observed an elderly male individual on the dock who was not present upon later inspection of the area. Individual appeared to be in possession of a thermos and a fishing line. Individual raised the thermos in the direction of the subject at approximately 9:23. Subject raised his hand in response. Individual was not present when operatives reached the dock. No vehicle was observed entering or leaving the parking area that could account for the individual's presence or absence.*

Voss set the report down.

Picked up her coffee.

Drank it.

Picked up her phone.

Put it down.

Looked at the report.

Somewhere in the building a door opened and closed and footsteps went past her office and the ordinary institutional Tuesday continued its business around her with the complete indifference of institutions to the fact that their frameworks were insufficient.

She picked up the report again.

Read the part about the elderly male individual one more time.

Filed it.

Opened the next item in her inbox.

The coffee was cold.

She didn't get up to make more.

Chapter 24

2:23 PM

SEEN: WHAT YOU ARE CHAPTER TWENTY-FOUR: DANIEL'S PAPER

It had been in the drawer since January.

Not hidden — Daniel didn't hide things, it wasn't in his nature, the making-room version of a person didn't hide things because hiding required the kind of interior management that was the opposite of making room. It was in the drawer the way important things were in drawers when you weren't sure what to do with them yet — present, accessible, waiting for the moment that would tell you what it was for.

He'd written it the night after the first river.

Two in the morning, Sarah asleep, the cabin quiet in the specific way cabins were quiet in January when the cold pressed against the windows and the woodstove was doing its work and the world outside had reduced itself to the essential. He'd sat at the kitchen table with a yellow legal pad and the specific urgency of a man who had experienced something he didn't have language for yet and understood that the language needed to be attempted before the experience became too familiar to see clearly.

He'd written it in forty minutes.

Read it back.

Folded it.

Put it in the drawer under the phone charger and the takeout menus and the various small items that accumulated in kitchen drawers across the life of a house and had not taken it out since except once, in March, to read it again to confirm it still said what he thought it said, which it did, and to return it to the drawer and close the drawer and go back to whatever he'd been doing.

The question of what to do with it had been running quietly underneath everything since January.

Not urgently. He wasn't a man who did things urgently unless urgency was the right instrument, and the paper hadn't felt like an urgency situation — it had felt like a patience situation, the specific kind of patience that wasn't waiting for a thing to happen but waiting to understand what a thing was for. The barn had been teaching him the difference between those two kinds of patience and he was learning it slowly and finding the learning worth the pace.

He knew it needed to go in the map.

Had known it since the night he wrote it, in the way you knew things before you were ready to do anything about them — the both-and of knowing and not-yet, the knowledge present and patient and willing to wait for the readiness to catch up.

The readiness arrived on a Sunday morning in late May.

He woke and lay in the early light and felt it — not dramatically, the quiet arrival of a thing that had been building to the surface and had found, on this particular Sunday morning, the surface.

Sarah was at the kitchen table when he came downstairs. The laptop open, the cursor blinking, her coffee in her left hand and the pen she still sometimes used in her right even though the laptop was right there, the habitual dual-instrument approach of a woman who had been writing herself into larger versions of herself for months and had developed her own methods for the work.

She looked up.

Read his face the way she read things — both kinds, the surface and the underneath.

"Morning," she said.

"Morning," he said.

He went to the drawer.

Took out the paper.

Set it on the table beside her laptop without explanation and went to pour his coffee and stood at the kitchen window looking at the May morning while she read it.

The tree line fully green now, the decision that had been suggested in April fully arrived, the world doing what it did when it finally committed to a season — completely, without qualification, the green of it dense and particular and entirely unlike the tentative green of April, the May green that knew what it was.

He heard her stop moving behind him.

The specific stillness of a person reading something that has required their full attention and is receiving it.

He drank his coffee.

Looked at the tree line.

Gave her the time it needed.

After a while she said: "Daniel."

Not a question. The specific way she said his name when it was carrying more than identification — the weight of something in it, the both-and of a name that had learned to mean several things simultaneously across the months of their living inside the same current.

He turned.

She was looking at the paper. Then at him. Then back at the paper with the expression of a woman who had been reading things for a long time and knew the difference between writing that was competent and writing that was true and was holding the latter in her hands.

"This has been in the drawer since January," she said.

"Yes."

"You wrote it the night of the first river."

"Yes."

She looked at him. "Why didn't you show me."

He thought about this honestly, which was the only way he thought about things that mattered. "I didn't know what it was for yet," he said. "I knew it was true. I didn't know what it was for."

She looked at the paper.

He crossed to the table and sat across from her and they were two people at a kitchen table on a Sunday morning in May with the green world outside and the coffee going warm between them and a single folded page of yellow legal pad that had been in a kitchen drawer since January.

"Read it to me," she said. "Out loud."

He looked at her.

"I want to hear you say it," she said. "In your voice. The way you wrote it."

He picked up the paper.

Read it.

The current was hers. I stood on the bank and felt it from a distance and understood that my version wasn't going in. My version was staying. Not from fear — from function. The river needs the bank. Without the bank it's flood. I am not the water. I am what the water runs beside and what that running shapes, and the shaping goes both ways, and I did not know this was a large thing until I was standing in it and found it was.

She waded in in December. I stood on the bank in January and felt the difference between watching someone be fully themselves and being fully yourself, and understood that the difference was not a failure of mine but a design — that the design required both, that someone had thought about this, that the both-and extended to the people in the large thing and not just to the large thing itself.

I don't know what I believe about who designed it. I know what it felt like to stand on the bank and feel the current from a distance and choose to stay on the bank not because I was afraid of the water but because the bank was where I was supposed to be. I know that the choosing felt like the large thing. I know that making room for something is not the same as being outside it.

I know that I love her. That's not the insight. The insight is that loving her and being the bank and making room and standing at the edge of the large thing she is wading through — these are not four different things. They are one thing. They are my version of the one thing.

I wrote this at two in the morning because I was afraid that by morning it would be too familiar to see clearly.

It is not too familiar. It is the clearest thing I have ever seen.

He set the paper down.

The kitchen was quiet.

Outside the May morning. The green world. The sound of a bird in the tree line doing its particular Tuesday — Sunday, he corrected himself — business with the cheerful indifference of a creature that had no concept of the weight of what had just been said in the kitchen it was nesting near.

Sarah was looking at him.

Not with the expression she wore when things were moving through her — not the frequency-receiving expression, not the open-receptive stillness she'd been learning at the river. The other expression. The one that was simply her, the full version of her, looking at him with the complete attention of a woman who knew what she had and knew it clearly.

"Daniel," she said.

"Yes."

"This goes in the map."

"I know," he said. "I knew when I wrote it."

"The person beside the catalyst in the next group," she said. "The person who stands on the bank while someone else wades in and has to find their own version of the large thing. They need to read this."

"I know," he said.

She looked at the paper on the table between them. Then at him. The May light coming through the kitchen window and landing on both of them in the generous way May light landed on things it liked.

"You've been the bank this whole time," she said. "Since December. The making-room version, the staying-on-the-bank version, the person who found their large thing in the standing rather than the wading." She paused. "I've been so inside my own version of this that I haven't said that clearly enough."

He looked at his coffee.

"You didn't need to," he said.

"I needed to," she said. "You needed to hear it." She leaned forward slightly across the table. "Daniel. What you wrote — the shaping goes both ways. You wrote that in January and it's been true since December and it's going to be true for every person who stands on a bank beside someone wading and wonders if the standing is the lesser thing."

He looked at her.

She held his eyes.

"It's not the lesser thing," she said. "It's the designed thing. The Weavers built the bank as carefully as they built the river. I know this the way I know the frequency at the river — both kinds, the surface and the underneath. You are part of the design."

He was quiet for a long moment.

The kitchen around them. The May morning outside. The paper on the table with its forty minutes of two in the morning honesty folded and unfolded and folded again and finally, on a Sunday in May, read aloud in the voice it had been written in, to the person it had been written near without knowing it was being written for her.

"The Weavers designed everything," he said. Slowly. Working through it. "The catalyst and the bank. The river and the thing that runs beside it."

"Everything," she said.

"Including this conversation."

"Probably," she said. "Almost certainly."

He looked at the paper.

Looked at her.

"They have a lot of nerve," he said.

She laughed — the real kind, the surprised kind, the laugh that arrived when something was exactly funny in exactly the right moment. He laughed with her, and the kitchen held the laughter the way the barn held Thursday nights — completely, with the quality of a space that had been asked to contain more than its dimensions suggested and was finding the asking entirely within its capacity.

The May morning outside.

The both-and in the kitchen.

Two people at a table with a piece of yellow legal paper and two coffees and the green world coming through the window and the Weavers present in the specific satisfied way they were present when a thing they'd designed was being used to its full capacity which was, Sarah was increasingly certain, their favorite thing.

She picked up the paper carefully.

Set it beside the laptop.

Opened a new document.

Began to type.

The map growing on a Sunday morning in May the way it grew every morning — one true thing at a time, the cursor patient, the blank page receiving what it was given with the specific generosity of something that had been waiting for exactly this and found the waiting entirely reasonable given what it was waiting for.

Daniel watched her type.

Drank his coffee.

Felt the current of her running alongside his in the May morning light — the river and the bank, the both-and of it present and specific and entirely designed, the design more interesting and more alive the further into it they went.

Outside a bird landed in the tree line and reconsidered and flew off somewhere more urgent.

The cursor blinked.

Sarah typed.

The map grew.

Chapter 25

2:27 PM

SEEN: WHAT YOU ARE CHAPTER TWENTY-FIVE: THE CIRCLE OVERFLOWS

It happened the way real things happened — not with announcement, not with a moment you could point to afterward and say *there, that's when it changed,* but gradually and then completely, the way rivers rose and the way seasons turned and the way barns became more than barns.

Word had spread.

Not through channels or campaigns or any of the mechanisms people used when they wanted things to spread. Through the specific urgency of person to person — the particular tone of someone who has found something they can't keep to themselves not because they're incapable of keeping things to themselves but because this specific thing was the kind of thing that insisted on being shared, that arrived with its own momentum, that moved through the people who had it toward the people who needed it with the patient inevitability of water finding its level.

Marcus had been adding chairs since April.

Not dramatically — one or two before a Thursday when the previous Thursday had left people standing at the back, then a row behind the circle when the one or two wasn't enough, then two rows, the barn's interior reorganizing itself around the growing fact of more people the way the barn reorganized itself around everything, with the accommodation of a space that had been asked to hold more than its walls suggested and was finding the asking within its capacity.

By the first Thursday in June the chairs were in rows behind the circle and people were still standing.

Marcus arrived at five on Thursday afternoon and set up every chair the barn contained and stood in the empty space and looked at what he'd built — the circle at the center, the rows expanding outward, the barn at its full capacity in a way that made the space feel not crowded but complete, the way a thing felt complete when it had finally found the scale it had always been designed for — and felt the frequency running through it all with the quality of a river that has been joined by so many tributaries that it has become something other than what it started as without ceasing to be itself.

He made coffee.

Set the kettle on.

Stood in the barn and let Thursday come.

They arrived in ones and twos and small groups.

The original circle first — filling their chairs with the ease of people who had somewhere they belonged and the belonging was specific and earned and required nothing further to justify it. Sarah and Daniel. Rachel and David. Emma with the container plans in her bag because the container problem was always present now, always slightly further along, the architectural mind never fully off the brief. Robert, who moved through the world differently than he had in January, the far-away quality replaced by something that was the opposite of far away — a specific presence, a quality of being entirely here that people who had not known him before noticed without being able to say exactly what it was they were noticing. James, whose compressed energy had been finding outlets in the Thursday nights, expanding into something that had started to look like the thing it had always been compressed toward.

Then the newer ones.

Carl with his wife.

He had brought her finally — the following Thursday after Don's first, the promise kept on schedule, Carl arriving with the woman he had lain beside for fifty-one years and felt as if for the first time in the dream's dark before dawn. She came in the way she did most things — without fuss, with complete attention, the specific quality of a woman who had been paying attention for fifty-one years and had no intention of stopping now.

She looked at the barn when she walked in. At the circle. At the people finding their chairs with the ease of belonging.

She looked at Carl.

He looked back.

She nodded once — the nod of a woman who had been waiting for her husband to find a room like this and was, now that he had, finding the room entirely adequate to the wait.

Maren had her tea ready.

Carl's wife looked at the cup and then at Maren and then at Carl and Carl said nothing because there was nothing useful to add and his wife, who had been reading him accurately for fifty-one years, read the nothing accurately.

"Ah," she said, and took the cup and sat down.

Don was already there with his wife, who had come the previous Thursday and spent the first forty minutes with the specific quality of a woman prepared to be politely unimpressed and had driven home afterward in a silence that Don had learned to read as the silence of someone whose framework had been significantly impacted and who required time to assess the damage.

She'd come back the following Thursday and brought her sister.

The sister had brought a colleague.

The colleague had apparently called three people.

This was how the barn had been filling — not a campaign, a contagion, the specific contagion of a thing that was real spreading the way real things spread, which was through the specific urgency of people who had encountered something true and found the encounter so thoroughly unlike what they'd expected that they needed to tell someone and the someone had needed to tell someone and so on until Marcus was setting up every chair the barn contained and people were still standing.

Diane arrived with her husband on the Thursday the chairs ran out.

She had come for the first time six weeks ago because her sister had insisted with the specific insistence of someone who has stopped being capable of not insisting, and Diane had spent her first Thursday certain it was a cult and her second Thursday crying without knowing why and her third Thursday calling her husband from the parking lot before she drove home.

You need to come, she'd said. *I can't explain it. You just need to come.*

He had come with the patient skepticism of a man who had been married to Diane for twenty-two years and had learned that when she said *you need to come* and couldn't explain why, the explanation arrived eventually and was usually worth waiting for.

He walked into the barn and found a seat in the second row and looked at the circle with the open assessment of a man who had not yet decided what he was looking at.

The frequency arrived.

He sat with it for a moment. Then another. His expression moving through several things in the way expressions moved when a framework encountered something it wasn't designed to accommodate — not collapsing, reassessing, finding the new load-bearing elements and redistributing the weight.

By the end of the evening he had the specific quality of a man who had driven to a thing his wife insisted on and found it to be not the thing he expected and to be, against all expectation, the thing he needed.

He didn't say this.

He said: "Same time next week?"

Diane looked at him.

"Yes," she said.

Peter had driven four hours.

This was the fact that most defined him to the circle when they eventually learned it — not who he was or what he did or any of the biographical information that people usually led with, but the four hours, the specific commitment of a man who had received a phone call from someone he hadn't spoken to in eleven years and had driven four hours on a Thursday because the voice on the phone had said *I can't explain it, just go, trust me* with the urgency of someone for whom the usual categories of explicable and inexplicable had been thoroughly reorganized and who needed him to get in the car.

He'd driven four hours.

Still skeptical when he arrived. Skepticism was his default instrument and he'd found it reliable and had no particular interest in replacing it with something less reliable. He'd sat in the back row with his arms crossed in the specific Carl-November posture of a man conducting an inspection and prepared to find things wanting.

The frequency had arrived by seven fifteen.

By eight he had uncrossed his arms.

By nine, when the gathering ended and people were finding their coats and finishing conversations, he was standing near the door talking to Robert with the specific quality of two people who had just discovered that they had been in different versions of the same place and were comparing notes with the urgency of travelers who have met unexpectedly far from home.

He drove four hours back.

Called the person who had called him from the road.

"I'm coming next Thursday," he said.

"I know," they said.

Chapter 26

SEEN: WHAT YOU ARE CHAPTER TWENTY-SIX: THE WOODS

Meridian sent a better team in mid-June.

Not because the previous teams had been inadequate — they had been adequate, professionally composed, operationally sound, filing reports that were models of careful language deployed in the service of describing things that careful language was not designed to describe. They had been adequate to every standard Meridian applied to field work and inadequate to the specific situation, which was a barn in Michigan that was doing something to surveillance equipment and personnel that the standards hadn't anticipated.

The better team was briefed extensively.

Voss had done the briefing herself, which was not standard — standard was a department head delegating to a team lead who delivered the operational parameters and the known anomalies and sent people into the field with the professional confidence of an organization that had encountered most things and developed protocols for most things and trusted the protocols.

She had done it herself because the known anomalies required a specific kind of framing that she wanted to control, which was the framing of: these things happened, they are documented, we do not know why they happened, you should be prepared for things to happen that you cannot explain, and your job is to document what you observe and return with the documentation regardless of what the documenting requires you to observe.

The team had listened with the professional composure of people who had been in the field long enough to have heard unusual briefings and who understood that unusual briefings preceded unusual assignments and that unusual assignments were, in their experience, usually explicable in retrospect even when they weren't explicable in the moment.

They were prepared.

They drove to the county road in two vehicles on a Thursday evening in mid-June when the light was still full at seven and the woods east of the barn were deep with the specific depth of Michigan hardwood forest in high summer — dark underneath the canopy, the undergrowth thick, the specific quality of a forest that had been doing its own business for a long time and found human presence neither threatening nor particularly interesting.

They positioned in the tree line at seven fifteen with the professional efficiency of a team that had done this many times and knew the choreography — the specific spacing, the equipment setup, the sightlines established, the communication protocols confirmed. Everything correct. Everything professional. The barn across the clearing with its high windows lit and the first cars pulling into the lot and the evening proceeding in the orderly fashion of a thing being properly managed.

For thirty minutes nothing unusual happened.

This was itself slightly unusual, given the operational history of this specific location, but the team was prepared for unusual and had been told to expect anomalies and so the absence of anomalies was itself an anomaly that they noted professionally and filed under: wait.

At seven forty-five the ants arrived.

Not a few ants. Not the ambient ant presence of a summer evening in a Michigan tree line, which was a known quantity that field operatives accounted for in the ordinary management of outdoor surveillance. A concentration that a naturalist would have found remarkable — the specific focused movement of a species that had been conducting its affairs on this planet for forty million years and had, in that time, refined its collective intelligence to a considerable degree and appeared to have applied that intelligence to the question of the team's boots.

The lead operative's boots specifically.

Then, with the patient thoroughness of a species that did not do things halfway, the rest of him.

The operative was a professional. He had been in difficult field conditions before. He had maintained his composure in circumstances that most people would not have maintained composure in and he intended to maintain it now, standing in a Michigan tree line on a Thursday evening in June with ants conducting what appeared to be a systematic and coordinated exploration of his person.

He maintained his composure for approximately ninety seconds.

Then he began moving in ways that were technically not running.

They were also not not-running.

The second operative — positioned twelve feet to the left, watching the lead operative's situation develop with the professional attention of someone who is grateful it is not happening to them and alert to the possibility that it might — began sneezing.

Not once. Not the ordinary sneeze of a person responding to a particular pollen or a particular moment of nasal irritation. The sustained sneezing of a biological process that had decided to express itself fully and completely and without reference to the professional requirements of the situation, each sneeze arriving with the unstoppable force of something that had been building since the operative had entered the tree line and had chosen this moment — the moment of the ants, the moment of the lead operative's technical-not-running — to present itself.

The sneezing achieved, within three minutes, a volume that was incompatible with the fundamental requirements of surveillance work.

It was, if one were keeping an objective record, extremely loud.

The third operative — whose assignment was the northwest quadrant, who had been watching the barn's parking lot with the focused attention of a professional and had thus far had the most unremarkable evening of anyone on the team — took two steps backward from his position to create distance from the sneezing and the ant situation and the technical-not-running and found, with the specific surprise of a person who has backed into something they did not know was behind them, a beehive.

Low in the branches. Established. The occupants, disturbed by the contact, responding with the focused collective attention of a colony that took its responsibilities seriously and had a well-developed sense of territorial boundaries and the willingness to enforce them.

The operative left his position.

Not in the technical-not-running manner. In the running manner.

The fourth operative, watching all three of these situations develop from her position in the southern quadrant with the expression of a professional who is witnessing the operational collapse of a well-planned field assignment and trying to determine the appropriate response, began writing in her notebook.

She wrote for two minutes.

Then a very large moth landed on her notebook.

Then another.

Then several more, with the patient unhurried accumulation of moths doing whatever moths did on June evenings in Michigan tree lines, which apparently included congregating with some enthusiasm on the notebook of surveillance operatives.

She looked at the moths.

The moths looked at her with the compound-eye authority of insects that had been doing this since before mammals were a concept and intended to continue doing it regardless of her documentation requirements.

She closed the notebook.

Singh was sitting on a log.

He had found the log in the first five minutes of the deployment — a fallen hardwood twenty yards back from the tree line, dry, stable, positioned in a small clearing where the canopy opened enough to let in the last of the evening light. He had assessed the log with the professional thoroughness of a man on his first field assignment and had determined that it was a good log and that his position on it gave him adequate sightlines to both the barn and his colleagues and that this was where he intended to be.

He was on his second field assignment for Meridian.

His first had been three weeks ago and had involved sitting in a vehicle outside a different barn in a different county and feeling, for the first time since joining the organization, that something about the organization's fundamental premise might require reexamination. He had filed his report and gone home and sat with the reexamination for three weeks with the methodical patience of a man who did not arrive at conclusions quickly but arrived at them thoroughly.

He had arrived at a conclusion.

He was sitting on his log with the conclusion present in his chest like the frequency he could feel from here — from twenty yards back in the tree line, through the trees and the clearing and the barn's timber walls, the frequency running at its register, warm and specific and entirely unlike anything his briefing had described as a threat.

His briefing had described it as a threat.

His briefing had described the group as a level-three management situation requiring observation, documentation, and assessment for potential escalation to intervention protocols. His briefing had described the frequency — not in those words, in the careful language of reports that described effects without naming causes — as evidence of coordinated psychological influence requiring counter-measures.

He sat on his log and felt the frequency from twenty yards and thought about his briefing.

He thought about Aaron.

Aaron, whose desk he occupied, whose files he had inherited, whose four-word resignation letter he had read on his first day — *I know what's happening* — and whose longer letter he had found in the secondary file folder, the one that said *I think you should know what you're actually doing*, which he had read three times and which had been, he now understood, the most useful piece of documentation in the entire file.

He knew what was happening.

He had known since his first assignment three weeks ago when he had sat in the vehicle and felt the frequency from outside the barn and understood, with the quiet clarity of something arriving completely, that the organization he had joined and the work he had been doing and the briefings he had been receiving were on the wrong side of the thing he was feeling.

He had been waiting for the right moment.

The right moment appeared to be now, with his colleagues dealing with ants and bees and moths and the sustained biological process of sneezing in the tree line, and the barn across the clearing doing what the barn did on Thursday nights, and the frequency present in his chest with the warm specific quality of something that had been expecting him.

He took out his phone.

Opened the email application.

Typed.

Not four words — he had read Aaron's four words and found them correct and insufficient. He typed the longer version, the one that said what he actually meant, which was: *I have been in the field for two assignments and I understand what this organization does and what it is trying to prevent and I believe it is wrong about what it is trying to prevent and I am going to the barn now.*

He sent it.

Put his phone in his pocket.

Stood up from his log.

Walked out of the tree line.

Crossed the clearing.

The frequency built with each step the way it built when you moved toward its source — not gradually, the specific building of something that recognized approach and responded to it, the warmth intensifying in the specific way of something that had been expecting this approach and found the expectation confirmed.

He reached the barn door.

Opened it.

The frequency arrived completely the moment he stepped inside — the full version, all at once, the warm everywhere quality of a barn that had been holding honest things for long enough that the holding had changed the nature of the space.

The circle was full.

There was a chair.

Maren was crossing the barn toward him with a cup of tea and the young-ancient eyes already on him with the expression of someone who had been expecting a specific person and had opinions about how long the specific person had taken to arrive.

She held out the cup.

He looked at it.

"How did you —" he started.

"You've been sitting on a log in the tree line for forty minutes," she said pleasantly. "A person develops preferences." She nodded at the chair. "Sit down, Singh."

He sat.

The frequency surrounded him with the complete warmth of something that had been waiting for him since the first assignment three weeks ago when he'd sat in the vehicle and felt it from outside and known — the quiet internal knowledge of a thing that had arrived completely — that the wrong side was the side he was on.

He was on the right side now.

The barn held Thursday.

The circle continued.

In the tree line, at some point, the ants concluded their assessment. The sneezing resolved. The bees returned to their hive with the settled authority of a colony whose territorial integrity had been adequately defended. The moths dispersed. The operatives regrouped with the professional composure available to people who had just experienced something their training had not addressed and who were going to have to write a report about it.

The report was going to be very difficult.

Outside the tree line and across the clearing in the lit barn, nobody heard any of it.

Maren, in her chair, looked at the high windows once with the small collegial smile she directed at things only she could see.

"Friends of yours," Sarah said quietly.

"Colleagues," Maren said, with the tone of someone giving credit where it was due. "They do excellent work."

"The ants," Sarah said.

"Among other things," Maren said.

Sarah looked at Singh in his chair across the circle — the new person, the frequency arriving in him with the visible quality it had in people for whom it was arriving for the first time, the specific expression of someone encountering something they had been feeling from a distance and are now inside and finding it larger than the distance suggested.

She felt his current.

The quality of a person who had made a decision and was sitting in the consequence of the decision and finding the consequence considerably better than the position they'd left.

She knew that quality.

She had worn it herself.

Once, in a barn, on a Thursday night, when everything had still been new and the frequency had been arriving for the first time and she hadn't yet known what any of it was or where it was going.

She looked at Maren.

Maren looked back with the young-ancient eyes carrying the specific warmth of someone who has seen this exact moment many times and finds it, every time, the best moment in the sequence.

The circle breathed.

The frequency ran.

Thursday continued its excellent work.

Chapter 27

2:46 PM

SEEN: WHAT YOU ARE CHAPTER TWENTY-SEVEN: THE PHANTOM TRAIN

The surveillance car followed Sarah on a Wednesday afternoon in late June.

Two operatives. Routine documentation. She was going to the farmer's market on Fifth Street, which she went to most Wednesdays when the season was right, which was not exciting work and was understood by both operatives to be not exciting work and was accepted with the professional equanimity of people who understood that not all assignments were the boat launch and that the farmer's market was considerably more likely to be the farmer's market than anything else.

The lead operative drove.

The second operative had the camera.

Sarah drove the route she always drove — out the cabin road, left on County Seven, through the light at Maple, down Fifth toward the market. The operatives followed at the standard distance, the camera logging the unremarkable footage of a woman driving to a farmer's market on a Wednesday afternoon in June, the kind of footage that filled report appendices and was reviewed by analysts who found nothing in it and noted the finding as: nothing unusual observed, subject proceeded to destination without incident.

At the intersection of Fifth and Marker the crossing signal began flashing.

Both operatives noted this. The crossing signal at Fifth and Marker was a known quantity — a railroad crossing that had not seen active rail service since 1987, the tracks pulled up in 1994, the signal itself a legacy infrastructure item that the county had never gotten around to removing and that occasionally malfunctioned in wet weather, which was documented in the operational notes for this route as: crossing signal may activate without cause, disregard.

The lead operative prepared to disregard it.

Then the train arrived.

Not the signal. Not the sound of a train at a distance becoming the sound of a train approaching. The train — present, enormous, moving from left to right across the intersection at a speed that was consistent with a freight train in transit, the sound of it filling the vehicle with the specific acoustic authority of several thousand tons of steel moving through space at considerable velocity.

The lead operative braked.

Hard.

The vehicle stopped.

The airbags deployed with the decisive enthusiasm of safety systems doing exactly what they had been designed to do in exactly the circumstances they had been designed for, which was the sudden deceleration of a vehicle in response to an imminent collision, the collision in this case being with a train that was crossing the intersection directly in front of them.

Both operatives sat in a cloud of deployment powder in the sudden silence.

Looked at the intersection.

The intersection was empty.

No train. No tracks — the tracks had been pulled up in 1994, the roadbed resurfaced, the crossing existing now only in the signal infrastructure and the operational notes and the specific cellular memory of an intersection that had once had trains and did not anymore.

The crossing signal was dark.

The Wednesday afternoon continued its business around the deployed-airbag vehicle with the complete indifference of a Wednesday afternoon that had not experienced anything unusual and saw no reason to adjust its behavior accordingly. A woman on a bicycle went past. A dog walker. The ordinary June afternoon of a small Michigan town going about its affairs.

Sarah's car was visible in the rearview mirror, having passed through the intersection on her way to the farmer's market, unaware that anything was occurring behind her.

The lead operative looked at the empty intersection for a moment.

Then at the airbags.

Then at the second operative.

The second operative looked back with the expression of a professional who has just experienced something that is going to be very difficult to document and is already composing the language.

"The signal malfunctioned," the lead operative said.

The second operative looked at the empty intersection where the train had been.

"Yes," she said.

"Visual anomaly," he said. "Consistent with equipment malfunction."

She looked at the airbags.

"The airbags deployed in response to the visual anomaly," he said, with the careful precision of a man constructing a report sentence by sentence and testing each one for professional defensibility before committing to it.

She looked at where the tracks weren't.

"Yes," she said.

They sat in the deployed-airbag vehicle in the middle of Fifth Street for another moment while the Wednesday afternoon continued around them. The dog walker came back the other direction. The woman on the bicycle had gone.

The lead operative took out his phone and called for a vehicle replacement.

The second operative opened her notebook.

Wrote the date and time.

Looked at what she'd written.

Turned to a fresh page.

Wrote the date and time again.

Looked at that.

Closed the notebook.

They sat.

"The farmer's market," the lead operative said finally.

"She's already there," the second operative said.

"Yes," he said.

They sat in the deployed-airbag vehicle on Fifth Street and did not go to the farmer's market because there was no longer a vehicle capable of going to the farmer's market and also because neither of them was entirely certain that going to the farmer's market was the appropriate next action following the events of the past four minutes, which had included a train that wasn't there and airbags that were.

The replacement vehicle arrived in twenty-two minutes.

They transferred the equipment.

Continued the documentation detail.

Found Sarah at the flower stall, buying dahlias, entirely unaware.

Filmed the dahlias.

Filed the report.

Sarah found out Thursday.

David had the report — not officially, through the specific channels that David had been maintaining since leaving his previous position, the careful cultivation of information flows that operated adjacent to official ones and were considerably more candid. He set it on the table during the pre-gathering coffee and the circle read it in the particular silence of people encountering documentation of something they had a stake in.

The report described the visual anomaly in the careful language Voss's division had developed for describing things it didn't have other language for. It described the airbag deployment. It described the empty intersection. It used the phrase *no physical evidence of rail infrastructure* which was, David noted, technically accurate and practically extraordinary given what the operatives had apparently experienced.

Rachel read this section twice.

"A train," she said. "That wasn't there."

"Since 1994," David said. "The tracks."

"They saw a train on tracks that don't exist," Rachel said, with the precision of someone stating the facts as they were rather than as they were comfortable to state.

"Yes," David said.

James said: "Was anyone hurt."

"Bruised," David said. "The airbags. Pride primarily."

The circle absorbed this.

Then Robert said, very quietly, with the specific quality of a man who had been somewhere else and come back and had opinions about the nature of what was possible: "The train was real."

The circle looked at him.

"To them," he said. "In that moment. At that intersection. The train was entirely real." He looked at his hands. "That's not a trick. That's not a malfunction. That's —" He paused. "That's a layer. A different layer becoming briefly visible in this one."

The barn held this.

Maren drank her tea with the expression of a woman hearing a student arrive at a conclusion she had been waiting for them to arrive at and finding the arrival satisfying.

"Like a ghost," Emma said. The architectural mind finding the closest available framework.

"Like a memory," Robert said. "The intersection remembering what it used to be. Being shown what it used to be." He looked at Maren. "They do that. The Weavers. Show things what they were."

"Sometimes," Maren said. "When it's useful."

"Was it useful," Rachel said, with the edge she kept available for things that required the edge.

Maren considered this with genuine deliberation. "Two operatives are sitting in a deployed-airbag vehicle on Fifth Street right now," she said, "reassessing the foundational premises of their professional lives." She drank her tea. "I find that useful, yes."

The circle was quiet for a moment.

Then James said, with the compressed dry energy that had been finding its outlet in Thursday nights for months: "They do love trains."

And the barn laughed.

The real kind. The releasing kind. The kind that arrived when something was genuinely funny and the room knew it simultaneously — the laugh of people who had been sitting with the accumulating absurdity of Meridian's operational history and had arrived at the train that wasn't there and found it the funniest thing in a sequence of increasingly funny things, each one more professionally inexplicable than the last, the whole sequence building to this specific Wednesday afternoon on Fifth Street with the airbags and the empty intersection and the two operatives sitting in the powder cloud of their own deployment looking at tracks that weren't there.

Marcus laughed with the releasing quality that the boat launch had begun in him — the real laugh, the physical laugh, the laugh of a man who had been patient for a long time about a great many things and was finding patience and laughter increasingly compatible.

Carl said: "Jesus Christ."

Which was exactly right.

Don said: "Does this kind of thing —" and gestured vaguely at the report "— happen a lot."

"It's escalating," David said, in the tone of a man reporting a trend he found professionally interesting and personally hilarious.

"Escalating," Don said.

"The early incidents were subtle," Rachel said. "Flat tires. Equipment anomalies. A GPS making questionable routing decisions."

"Marcus's truck," Carl said.

"Yes," Rachel said. "Then the drone landing itself. The mathematical pattern on the audio." She looked at the report. "Now a train."

Don looked at Carl.

"You could've warned me," he said.

"I did warn you," Carl said.

"You said it was interesting," Don said.

"It is interesting," Carl said.

Don looked at the report one more time.

"That's one word for it," he said.

The barn laughed again — the second wave, the laugh that arrives when the first laugh has opened the room enough that the second one can be larger — and Maren looked at the high windows with the collegial expression and the warm acknowledgment of something that found Thursday nights exactly as satisfying as advertised.

Sarah looked at the report in David's hand. At the clinical language describing a train that wasn't there. At the airbag deployment noted with professional composure. At the phrase *no physical evidence of rail infrastructure* sitting in the middle of a paragraph about two operatives seeing a train on non-existent tracks on a Wednesday afternoon while she was buying dahlias.

She thought about the farmer's market.

The dahlias on the kitchen table.

The ordinary Wednesday afternoon she had driven through without knowing that behind her something impossible was happening in the service of her Thursday nights.

She thought about what Robert had said.

The intersection remembering what it used to be. Being shown what it was.

She thought about the map. About what she was writing every morning. About the both-and of a character writing and being written, the river and the bank, the being-read while reading.

She thought about what it meant that the Weavers could show an intersection its own past so completely that two trained professionals braked for a train that had been gone for thirty years.

She thought about what they could show a person.

Filed it.

Both kinds.

Both real.

Maren was finishing her tea when Sarah looked at her.

"They do love trains," Sarah said.

Maren looked at the high windows with the expression of someone acknowledging a design preference in colleagues whose work she respected.

"They love anything with momentum," she said. "Trains. Rivers." She set down her mug. "Stories."

She said it the way she said things that were more than they appeared — plainly, without performance, the specific plainness of something that was accurate and was being stated accurately and was going to sit in the room and do its work without requiring any assistance from emphasis or explanation.

Stories.

Sarah looked at her.

Maren looked back.

The young-ancient eyes saying something that wasn't words and had been saying it since the first Thursday and was saying it more clearly now, here, in the full barn on a Thursday night in June with the frequency running at its deepest register and the circle full and Singh in his chair and Estelle in the second row and the train that wasn't there filed in the report on the table.

Both kinds.

Both real.

Sarah looked at the window.

The June dark outside.

The barn around her.

The map on the laptop on the kitchen table three miles away with the cursor patient and the document open and twenty-three pages of it already written and more arriving every morning.

Stories, she thought.

With momentum.

She filed it where she filed things that were becoming speakable.

Not yet.

But soon.

Chapter 28

2:57 PM

SEEN: WHAT YOU ARE CHAPTER TWENTY-EIGHT: VOSS READS THE REPORTS

She did it on a Sunday.

Not a workday — deliberately not a workday, the specific choice of a woman who had been reading the file in portions on workdays for months and had understood, sometime around the phantom train report, that reading it in portions on workdays was itself a management strategy and that the management strategy was no longer adequate to what the file had become.

She needed to read it beginning to end.

She needed to read it on a day when there was no next item in the inbox waiting, no meeting to prepare for, no operational requirement providing the professional context that had been allowing her to process each report as a discrete item rather than as part of the accumulation it was part of.

She brought it home on a Friday.

Left it on the kitchen table over Saturday.

On Sunday morning she made coffee — a full pot, the deliberate preparation of someone settling in for a long sitting — and sat down at the kitchen table and opened the file.

Read it from the beginning.

The beginning was unremarkable.

This was the thing she'd forgotten — how unremarkable the beginning was, how completely the early reports had the quality of routine level-three documentation, the careful professional language of a division that had encountered this kind of situation before and had protocols for it and was applying the protocols with the methodical patience of an organization that trusted its methods.

Subject: Sarah Mitchell. Age forty-three. Divorced, finalized. Relocated to rural Antrim County following separation. No prior flags. No known associations with flagged individuals or organizations. Came to attention through a standard referral from a regional affiliate following a reported incident at a community gathering.

She read the incident report. The barn on the county road. The gathering. The initial assessment: level-three, monitoring recommended, no immediate intervention required. Standard.

She read the first three months of surveillance reports.

They were exactly what they appeared to be. A woman finding her footing after a significant life change. A social circle forming around a weekly gathering. Nothing that the protocols hadn't seen before. Nothing that the protocols weren't designed to manage.

She drank her coffee.

Turned the page.

The file changed in January.

Not dramatically — the specific quality of a change that was visible in retrospect and had not been visible in the individual reports as they arrived, the accumulation becoming something different from the sum of its parts in the way that accumulations sometimes did when the parts were building toward something the framework wasn't tracking.

The boat launch incident was January.

She read it again — the GPS rerouting, the truck in the water, the two operatives standing in the shallows with their ruined shoes and their insufficient reports. She had read this report six times since it was filed and each time had processed it as an isolated anomaly and filed it under: investigate further, no immediate action required.

Reading it now in sequence — after the first three months of entirely ordinary surveillance and the emerging pattern of small irregularities and the frequency appearing at the edges of reports as a description of something the operatives couldn't name — she read it differently.

Not as an isolated anomaly.

As the first thing that hadn't been managed.

She sat with this.

The January light coming through her kitchen window, the ordinary Sunday morning of her kitchen, the coffee pot on the counter and the neighbor's dog doing something in the yard next door and the entirely ordinary domestic Sunday proceeding around her while she sat at the kitchen table and read the file from the beginning and understood, for the first time, what she was reading.

She turned the page.

February.

The dreams. The operatives with the headaches and the vivid dreams, uncoordinated, independently, same forty-eight-hour window. She had read each of these reports individually and noted the coincidence and flagged it for follow-up and the follow-up had produced nothing except a medical assessment that found both operatives fit for duty and a notation in their files that the dreams were unrelated to operational exposure.

She read them in sequence now.

The same forty-eight-hour window.

The specific quality of the dreams as described by both operatives in the stilted careful language of professionals describing something they were embarrassed to be describing — the warmth, the specific warmth both of them mentioned, the specific word both of them used independently in reports written without coordination.

She had not noticed, reading them separately, that both of them used the same word.

She noticed now.

She turned the page.

The drone.

The flat tires — three of them, same vehicle, no mechanical cause found on inspection. The operative who called his mother. The budget line that vanished without notation, present in January and absent in February, no paperwork, no approval, no explanation.

She read these in sequence and felt the accumulation differently than she'd felt the individual reports.

Not isolated anomalies.

A pattern.

Not the pattern the file was designed to track — the pattern the file had been assembled around was the group and its activities and the potential escalation of those activities beyond acceptable thresholds. That pattern was present in the file and she had been reading it faithfully for months.

The other pattern — the one she hadn't been tracking, the one that had been building in the margins of the file she was tracking, in the anomalies and the equipment malfunctions and the operative who called his mother and the dreams and the budget line that disappeared — that pattern was different.

That pattern was not about the group.

That pattern was about what happened to the people and equipment that tried to observe the group.

She sat back.

Drank her coffee.

It was getting cold.

She drank it anyway.

Looked at the file.

Turned the page.

March.

The mathematical pattern on the audio recording. She read the analyst's report again — the careful stepping-stone language, the seventeen eliminated sources, the four diagnostic runs, the eleven environmental variables — and read the final paragraph again.

The recording appears to contain a recurring mathematical structure consistent with intentional signal generation, for which no known intentional source has been identified.

She had read this paragraph many times.

She had never read the sentence that followed it — the sentence she had, she now understood, been reading past rather than reading, the sentence that required the paragraph before it and the full file before both of them to mean what it meant.

The pattern's characteristics suggest the presence of a signal operating in a frequency range for which current instrumentation was not designed, and is detecting incidentally.

Detecting incidentally.

The equipment picking up something it wasn't designed to detect because the something existed in a range the design hadn't accounted for. Not because the something was subtle or rare or exceptionally difficult to find — because the instrumentation had been built in a world that didn't know the something existed and had therefore built nothing to find it.

She sat with this for a long time.

The coffee cold in the cup.

The Sunday morning around her.

April.

The grocery store incident. She read it again — the address in the promotional code, the specific format matching David's documentation style, the Indiana facility address appearing inside a cereal box that Sarah hadn't usually bought. She had read this report and found it inexplicable and filed it under inexplicable and moved on.

She read it now in the sequence of everything before it and felt something she had not felt reading it the first time, or the second time, or the fifth time.

She felt it as communication.

Not malfunction. Not coincidence. Not the kind of inexplicable that required investigation so it could be explained away.

Communication.

Something had put an address in a cereal box that a woman had been moved to choose on a Wednesday in the cereal aisle of a grocery store, and the address had been a Meridian facility, and the communication had been — she sat with the word — *we know.*

We know where you are.

We know what you're doing.

We are not impressed.

She set the report down.

Picked it up again.

She had been reading this file for months as the documentation of a surveillance operation. She was reading it now as the documentation of a conversation — a conversation she had not known she was in, between her organization and something that found her organization's activities noted, assessed, and untroubling.

The cold coffee.

She got up.

Made more.

Stood at the kitchen counter while it brewed and looked at the ordinary Sunday morning outside her window — the neighbor's yard, the dog, the quiet street, the entirely unremarkable suburban Sunday proceeding without awareness of the woman standing at the counter who was rereading her professional life and finding the reread significantly different from the original reading.

She poured the coffee.

Sat back down.

Turned the page.

May.

The phantom train.

She read it slowly this time. Not the clinical language — underneath the clinical language, the thing the clinical language was describing. Two operatives. A crossing signal. A train on tracks that had been removed in 1994. Airbags. The cloud of deployment powder. The empty intersection.

The elderly male individual on the dock.

She stopped.

She had read the boat launch report six times. She had not, she now understood, fully read it. She had read the truck in the water and the two operatives in the shallows and had processed these as the anomaly and had moved on. She had read the notation about the elderly male individual and had filed it under: unidentified bystander, no relevance determined.

She turned back.

Found the boat launch report.

Found the notation.

Individual was observed on the dock upstream. Individual raised a coffee thermos in the direction of the subject. Subject raised a hand in response.

She turned back to the phantom train report.

Found the notation.

An elderly male individual on a bench approximately thirty yards from the intersection was observed prior to the incident. Individual was not present upon inspection following the incident. No vehicle was observed.

She turned back.

Found the Meridian building report from February. The one about the janitor.

An individual was observed in Conference Room B corridor whose name does not appear in building personnel records. Individual made a statement before leaving: "You might want to consider that you're on the wrong side of this."

She set all three reports on the table side by side.

The elderly male individual.

The dock. The intersection. The conference room corridor.

Three different locations. Three different months. Three different operatives filing three different reports. The same individual described in the same terms — old, unhurried, present without apparent purpose, absent without apparent departure.

She looked at the three reports on her kitchen table.

The coffee was hot this time.

She drank it.

Thought about the wrong side.

Thought about Aaron's longer letter, which she had been carrying in the file under a section labeled *personnel* and which she had been reading with the specific frequency of something she couldn't stop returning to — the letter that said *I think you should know what you're actually doing* and that she had filed under: disgruntled former employee, review at annual assessment, and had been rereading approximately once a week since February.

She thought about Singh's resignation email.

I have been in the field for two assignments and I understand what this organization does and what it is trying to prevent and I believe it is wrong about what it is trying to prevent and I am going to the barn now.

She looked at the three reports side by side on her kitchen table.

She looked at Sarah's photograph, which she had brought home with the file and which was in the upper right corner of the spread the way it was in the upper right corner of the file folder, the photograph that she had been looking at for months with the expression she didn't have a professional category for.

What are you, she had thought at the photograph. Repeatedly. With increasing frequency. With the increasing understanding that the question was the right question and that the answer was not in any report she had filed or would file.

She looked at the three elderly-male-individual notations.

She looked at the photograph.

She thought about the founder standing in a river.

She thought about the word the founder had used — *Weavers* — and then hadn't used, had pulled back from, had replaced with the careful operational language of an organization that had built itself specifically to not use words like that.

She thought about what it meant that the same individual appeared in three separate reports filed by three separate operatives in three separate locations across four months.

She thought about what it meant that the individual had said *wrong side* to a conference room corridor and raised a thermos at a man whose truck was in a river and been present at an intersection where a train that no longer existed had stopped two of her operatives.

She sat at her kitchen table on a Sunday morning with the full file spread in front of her and the coffee hot and the ordinary suburban Sunday proceeding outside her window and felt the framework doing what it had been doing for months — developing cracks at a rate that exceeded its ability to repair them — and understood, reading the file from the beginning for the first time, that the cracks were not in the framework.

The cracks were in her.

The framework was fine.

She was the one who was changing.

She sat with this for a long time.

The file spread on the table.

The coffee cooling again.

Three reports side by side.

The photograph of Sarah Mitchell in the upper right corner, looking out of it with the expression Voss had been trying to categorize for seven months and had not been able to categorize because the expression was not in any category she had built and was not going to be, because the expression was simply a woman who knew what she was and had stopped apologizing for it and was looking at the camera with the full version of herself entirely present and entirely without management.

Voss looked at the photograph for a long time.

Then she looked at the three reports.

Then she picked up her phone.

Called the founder.

"I read the full file," she said. "Beginning to end."

The founder was quiet for a moment. "And."

"The individual," she said. "The elderly male. He appears in three separate reports. Three separate locations. Four months."

The founder was quiet for a longer moment.

"Yes," they said.

"You know who he is," Voss said.

Not a question.

The founder was quiet for the longest moment yet — the quality of quiet that contained a great deal that was not being said and was not going to be said on a phone call on a Sunday morning.

"Come to the barn Thursday," the founder said.

Voss looked at the photograph.

At the three reports.

At the full file spread across her kitchen table on a Sunday morning while the ordinary world proceeded outside her window entirely unaware.

"All right," she said.

She set the phone down.

Looked at the file.

Closed it.

Sat with the closed file and the hot coffee and the Sunday morning for a long time.

Then she opened it again.

Read the three reports one more time.

Set them down.

Said, to the empty kitchen, to the photograph, to the elderly male individual who appeared in three separate reports and had said *wrong side* to a conference room corridor:

"I'm beginning to think you're right."

The kitchen held this.

The coffee cooled.

Outside the ordinary Sunday.

Inside a woman sitting at the end of twenty years of professional certainty, reading a file that had been trying to tell her something since January, finally listening.

Chapter 29

SEEN: WHAT YOU ARE CHAPTER TWENTY-NINE: THE FOUNDER AT SARAH'S RIVER

They found it without difficulty.

This did not surprise them. Rivers of this kind announced themselves to people who knew what to listen for, and whatever else the founder had spent twenty-three years becoming, they had not become someone who could no longer hear water. The covered thing had been orienting toward rivers since January — since Voss had first mentioned the river in the file, since the photograph of Sarah standing in it had appeared in the surveillance report with the quality of a woman who had waded in and found something and was still finding it — and it oriented now with the compass certainty of something that recognized its own element.

They drove the county road in the early evening of a Thursday in late June.

Not to attend the barn — not yet, the barn was for later, the barn was the step after this one, and the founder had learned in twenty-three years of building an organization around the management of sequences that the steps had an order and the order mattered.

The river first.

They found the cabin road. Parked at the end of it where the gravel widened and the path into the tree line began. Got out. Stood for a moment in the June evening with the light still in the sky and the air carrying the specific quality of June evenings in northern Michigan — warm, particular, the smell of the tree line and the river beneath it, the sound of the water audible from here.

The covered thing arrived immediately.

Not the bank version — the full version, here, before the river was even visible, the frequency of this specific stretch of water already present in the air the way the barn's frequency was present in the barn's air, accumulated, structural, changed by what had been happening near it for months.

Someone had been standing in this river.

Regularly. With the full version of themselves. The frequency of it had soaked into the landscape the way the barn's frequency had soaked into the barn's timber — present whether anyone was here to feel it or not, the river having been in conversation with something that had changed the quality of the conversation's location.

They walked the path.

The root that caught your toe if you weren't watching — they stepped over it carefully, which was not how they would have walked this path twenty-three years ago, when they had walked paths like this without watching because they were twenty-nine and the path and the river and the full version of everything were all present simultaneously and required no management. Now they stepped carefully. Twenty-three years of careful.

The trees stepping back where the path widened.

The willows.

The river.

They stopped at the bank.

The covered thing came up against the sound of the water like a hand pressed flat against glass — the same response as their own river, the same compass-finding-north quality, the same involuntary orientation of something that had been held back from water for twenty-three years and recognized, again, what it had been held back from.

But different.

Their own river had felt like memory. The ache of something known and absent. The grief of a path not taken preserved in the landscape of the place where it hadn't been taken.

This river felt like evidence.

The specific quality of a place where someone had been choosing, every morning, the path they had chosen not to take — choosing it and wading in and standing in the full version and choosing it again and wading in again, the choosing accumulating in the water and the bank and the willows and the path the way all sustained choices accumulated in the places where they were made.

They stood at the bank and felt the evidence of Sarah's choosing and felt the covered thing respond to it with the specific response of something that had been shown what it had been avoiding and found the showing — not comfortable, not easy, something better than both.

True.

The river was running warm in the June evening, the summer pace of it, clear and purposeful and entirely certain of its direction. The willows overhead making their full green ceiling, the light coming through them in the particular way June light came through willows — softened, moving, the specific quality of this light at this hour in this place that existed nowhere else and that the covered thing recognized with the recognition that preceded consciousness.

They took off their shoes.

Stood in the grass.

The warm ground under their feet, the June grass, the river ten feet in front of them and the covered thing enormous and patient and the both-and of twenty-three years pressing on one side and the river on the other and them standing between the two in their bare feet in the June evening.

They had not been barefoot near water since the year they were twenty-nine.

They stood in the grass for a long time.

Felt the Weavers.

Not the way Sarah felt them — not the everywhere warmth, not the laughter at the edge of hearing, not the full frequency of a person who had been standing in the water for months and had the Weavers present in her life the way weather was present. The faint version. The covered thing's version. The frequency pressing through twenty-three years of management with the patient quality of something that had never stopped being there, that had been present on the other side of the coverage all along, waiting with the specific patience of something that operated on a longer timeline than the person doing the covering and had found the patience reasonable.

They felt the Weavers feel them back.

Not with the warmth Sarah described. With something quieter and more specific — the attention of something that had been waiting for this person to stand in this grass in this evening for a considerable time and was, now that it was happening, entirely present for the happening.

Not glad in the way the Weavers were glad when the boat launch worked or the train arrived at the intersection. Something older than glad. Something that had watched a person walk away from the full version of themselves twenty-three years ago and had been patient since and was now standing in the grass on the other side of the patience, feeling the person standing in the grass ten feet from the river, and was —

Still.

The Weavers, for once, were still.

The founder felt the stillness and understood it without being able to say how they understood it — the stillness of something that had been moving toward this moment for a very long time and had arrived at it and was letting the arrival be what it was without rushing the next thing.

They looked at the river.

The current running clear and warm in the June evening, moving through the willows' light and going on, going on, entirely certain and entirely indifferent and entirely itself.

They thought about Sarah wading in.

Not the photograph — they had the photograph, had been looking at the photograph for months with the expression Voss couldn't categorize. The other version. The version from the file's surveillance footage, the January morning, Sarah walking the path behind the cabin in the pre-dawn dark and wading into the December river with the specific quality of a woman who had decided something and was acting on the decision without ceremony.

They had watched that footage three times.

Each time they had watched it they had felt the covered thing respond — the compass-finding-north quality, the orientation toward what was on the screen, the involuntary recognition of something the coverage couldn't entirely suppress.

They had filed the footage and moved on.

They had been filing things and moving on for twenty-three years.

The covered thing had been responding and waiting for twenty-three years.

They looked at the water.

The step between the grass and the river was ten feet.

Ten feet and twenty-three years.

They did not take the step.

Not tonight. Not yet. The bank was the honest position — Daniel's position, they understood now, reading the map that David had shared with the founder through channels that were complicated and worth the complication, the page about the river and the bank and the function of staying. They were not the river. They had never been the river. They were the covered thing and the covering and twenty-three years of an organization built to justify the covering and the exhaustion of the justification and the grass under their bare feet in the June evening.

What they were was someone standing at the edge of the thing they had walked away from.

That was enough for tonight.

That was more than they had done in twenty-three years.

They stood until the light went out of the sky and the June dark came in warm and full and particular and the river ran on with its complete indifference and the willows went dark overhead and the Weavers remained still in the specific stillness of something attending a moment it has been patient toward.

Then they put their shoes back on.

Walked back up the path.

Stepped over the root.

Got in their car.

Sat.

The river audible from here. The covered thing enormous and patient and changed in its character from the car-drive version — less covered, the June evening and the grass and the ten feet and the twenty-three years having done something to the coverage that the coverage would not recover from.

Good, they thought, with the specific conviction of someone deciding something they had been deciding toward for a long time and have finally arrived at. Good that it won't recover.

They thought about Thursday.

The barn. The circle. The frequency Voss had been describing in her reports with increasing inadequacy since February, the frequency that left mathematical signatures on surveillance equipment, the frequency that was large enough to feel from the parking lot.

They thought about Sarah.

The woman in the photograph who had gotten further than anyone in twenty-three years. Who had waded in in December and kept wading. Who was writing the map every morning on a silver laptop that had arrived through channels the founder was only beginning to understand.

They thought about what the founder had felt standing at the river's edge.

The evidence of someone's choosing accumulated in the landscape.

What would it feel like to be the one doing the choosing instead of the one building the organization to prevent the choosing.

They had known what it felt like.

Once.

They sat in the car until the dark was complete and the river was sound rather than sight and the covered thing had settled into the level it had found at the bank — the honest level, the neither-managing-nor-arriving level, the level of someone standing at the edge of the water in their bare feet on a June evening and telling the truth about where they were.

Not in the water.

At the edge.

Both-and.

They started the engine.

Drove back toward town through the June dark with the window down and the warm air coming in and the covered thing at its honest level in their chest and the specific understanding that had been forming since the car ride to their own river and had arrived, tonight, at the bank of Sarah's river, complete:

The thing they had built Meridian to prevent was not preventable.

It had never been preventable.

It was what people were when they stopped covering it.

And it had been waiting, with the patience of rivers and Weavers and the elderly male individual on his rock, for them to stop.

They drove.

The June dark around them.

The barn on Thursday.

The step not taken tonight available on the other side of Thursday.

The river still running behind them, warm in the June dark, moving through the willow light and going on.

Going on.

Always going on.

Chapter 30

SEEN: WHAT YOU ARE CHAPTER THIRTY: THE MERIDIAN MEETING

The meeting was called for Tuesday.

Not by Voss — by the founder, which was itself unusual enough that Voss had noted it in her calendar with the specific notation she used for things that represented departures from established pattern: *founder attending in person. First time since org review, March two years ago.*

The founder had not attended an operational meeting in person in two years.

The team assembled in Conference Room B at nine in the morning with the collective composure of professionals who had been doing difficult work for a long time and had learned to bring their full operational capacity to whatever the day required regardless of who was in the room.

The founder sat at the head of the table.

Voss sat to their left with the full file and the Sunday morning still present in her somewhere underneath the professional composure — the kitchen table, the three reports side by side, the cold coffee, the photograph. She had come to the meeting differently than she had come to any meeting in twenty years of this work. Not with the framework fully operational. With the framework present and the cracks in it visible to her in a way they had not been visible before Sunday and that she was not yet sure what to do with.

She had decided, sitting at the kitchen table on Sunday morning, that she would do nothing with them yet. That she would come to the meeting and present the file and watch the founder and wait.

She was good at waiting.

Twenty years had made her good at waiting.

She presented the file.

The recent reports first — the phantom train, the woods deployment, Singh's resignation. She presented these with the professional composure available to a woman who had read the full file from the beginning on a Sunday morning and was now presenting its contents to the person who had built the organization the file belonged to, watching their face while they read.

The founder read.

The phantom train report first. She watched their face while they read it and saw — not much, the founder had twenty-three years of not showing much, but underneath the professional surface the covered thing responding to the reports the way it had been responding to things since the June evening at the river, the compass-finding-north quality visible in small movements of expression that twenty years of reading people had given Voss the ability to catch.

Singh's resignation email next.

The founder read it twice.

Set it down.

Said nothing.

Voss presented the summary assessment. The operational history. The frequency in the audio equipment. The mathematical pattern. The accumulated anomalies across seven months of surveillance. The group's growth — from twelve to thirty-plus, the barn overflowing, the circle expanding by word of mouth in the specific way that things spread when they were real. The map Sarah was writing. The container Emma was designing.

She presented these things with the professional composure of a woman presenting a file and watched the founder receive them with the covered thing responding to each item in the specific way of something that recognized what it was hearing.

The department heads around the table listened and asked the questions that department heads asked and received the answers and had the expressions of professionals encountering a situation that exceeded the available protocols and were looking to the head of the table for the direction the protocols were insufficient to provide.

The founder looked at the file.

At Sarah's photograph.

The two fingers at the photograph's edge — the small unconscious gesture Voss had been watching since the rental house kitchen in April, the gesture of someone touching something they recognized.

The room waited.

The janitor came in at ten fifteen.

Not the building's janitor — Voss had worked in this building for eleven years and knew the building's janitor, whose name was Frank and who was sixty-one and had a daughter at Michigan State and pushed his cart with the specific rhythm of a man who had been doing the same route for so long that the route had become him and he had become the route.

This was not Frank.

This was an old man with a broom who moved through the room with the unhurried ease of someone for whom the room was not an obstacle to navigate but a landscape to inhabit, the specific quality of a person who belonged in any space they entered not because the space had been prepared for them but because they carried the belonging with them.

He pushed the broom along the far wall.

Nobody at the table reacted.

This was the thing Voss noted — the professional composure of a room full of experienced people not reacting to the arrival of an unknown individual during a closed operational meeting, the specific non-reaction of people who had been trained to manage their responses to unexpected things and were managing.

She reacted internally.

She had seen the notations in the file. The dock. The intersection. The corridor outside this room. She recognized the quality of his unhurried presence the way you recognized something you'd been reading about and had finally encountered in person — the recognition that was different from meeting something for the first time, the recognition that was confirming something you already knew.

He swept.

Moved toward the table.

The founder was looking at the file and had not looked up.

He swept near the table.

Swept past it.

Voss watched his face.

He was looking at the reports on the table — at the phantom train report, at Singh's resignation, at the operational history of seven months of Meridian encountering something it wasn't designed to encounter — and his expression was the expression she had been trying to categorize since the first notation in the dock report and had not been able to categorize because the expression was not one she had encountered in twenty years of reading faces in professional contexts.

It was the expression of someone reading something they had written.

Not reviewing a report. Reading their own work. The specific quality of a writer encountering their own sentences in the world — the recognition that was deeper than familiarity, the recognition of something that had come from inside you and gone out into the world and was now here in the world being what it was, and finding it, against the anxiety of every person who has put something into the world, better than they feared.

He made a small sound.

Not quite a laugh. The sound a person made when something on a page was exactly right — private, genuine, the sound of someone alone with a thing that had worked.

Voss looked at the founder.

The founder had looked up.

Was looking at the janitor.

And the founder's face was doing something Voss had never seen it do in eleven years of working for them — something that was not the professional surface and was not the covered thing straining against the professional surface and was not the grief and recognition of the photograph and was not the hope she had caught once in the rental house kitchen and filed under: misread, revise.

The founder's face was doing something that required no revision.

The founder was reading the name tag.

Voss looked at the name tag.

She could not read it from her position — the angle was wrong, the font small, the distance across the conference room table too great for the casual reading of a small name tag on a maintenance uniform.

The founder could read it.

She watched them read it.

Watched something move through the founder's face at the reading — the covered thing, enormous, the compass-finding-north quality fully present, not managed, not covered, fully present and responding to whatever was on the name tag with the recognition of something that had been waiting to recognize it for a very long time.

The janitor reached the door.

Stopped.

Did not turn around.

"You might want to consider," he said pleasantly, to the room, to the table, to the reports spread across it and the people around it and the twenty-three years of an organization built to manage what was in those reports, "that you're on the wrong side of this."

He pushed the broom out the door.

The room held the silence of eight professionals sitting with something that had no professional response available.

Voss did not look at the door.

She looked at the founder.

The founder was still looking at the door.

The covered thing enormous in their face, uncovered, the professional surface entirely insufficient for what was moving through it — recognition, grief, the complicated species of hope she had caught once and the thing that was not hope and was not grief and was not recognition but was some combination of all three that she had been trying to name since Sunday morning and was naming now:

Acknowledgment.

The founder was acknowledging something.

Not to the room. Not to Voss. To whatever had just left through the door, to whatever had been in the building in this corridor before and on the dock in January and at the intersection in June and in every margin of every significant thing that had happened in the file spread across the conference room table.

Acknowledging it.

The room waited.

The founder looked at the table. At the file. At Sarah's photograph with the two fingers at its edge.

Then they looked at Voss.

"The name tag," Voss said quietly.

The founder looked at her.

"What did it say," Voss said.

The founder was quiet for a long moment.

Then: "It said the same thing it always says," they said. "In every room. In every building. In every margin of every significant thing." They looked at Sarah's photograph. "It says what he is."

"Which is," Voss said.

The founder looked at the door.

"The one who writes the room," the founder said. "While the room is happening."

Voss sat with this.

The conference room around her — the table, the reports, the eight professionals who had the collective expression of people whose framework had just received information it was going to require considerable time to process.

"Thursday," the founder said.

"The barn," Voss said.

"Yes."

She looked at the file. At the photograph. At the door the janitor had pushed his broom through.

"All right," she said.

The meeting continued.

It covered the remaining operational items with the professional composure of people who had been trained to proceed regardless of circumstances and were proceeding. Reports were presented. Assessments were made. Actions were assigned.

Nobody mentioned the janitor.

This was not avoidance — it was the specific professional courtesy of a room full of people who understood that some things required private processing before they could be made institutional, and that the janitor was one of those things, and that the processing would happen in whatever time it required and the institutional response, if there was one, would follow.

Voss closed the meeting at eleven thirty.

The room emptied.

She sat at the empty conference room table with the file in front of her and the door the janitor had used still closed and the ordinary Tuesday morning institutional sounds of the building proceeding outside in the corridor.

She thought about the name tag.

She had not been able to read it.

She thought about the founder's face reading it.

She thought about *the one who writes the room while the room is happening.*

She thought about the file — seven months of a surveillance operation that had been, she now understood completely, also something else. Also a record of something writing a room. The barn writing itself onto the surveillance equipment. The river writing itself onto the people who stood in it. The frequency writing itself onto everything that tried to observe it without understanding what it was observing.

The old man on the dock with his thermos.

In the corridor.

At the intersection.

Writing.

She looked at Sarah's photograph.

The woman who had gotten further than anyone in twenty-three years.

The woman who was writing a map every morning on a silver laptop.

She thought about what it meant that the map and the surveillance file were both, in their different ways, records of the same thing.

She thought about what it meant to be written.

She thought about the wrong side.

She closed the file.

Picked up her phone.

Called the founder.

"Thursday," she said.

"Yes," the founder said.

"I'll be there," she said.

She set the phone down.

Looked at the conference room.

The empty chairs. The table. The reports she would file and the notations she would make and the operational record she would maintain with the professional composure of a woman who had been doing this work for twenty years.

And underneath all of that, running through all of it the way the river ran through the landscape it moved through, the frequency she had been reading about for seven months and had not yet felt directly and was going to feel Thursday and knew it and was, against twenty years of professional certainty, looking forward to the knowing.

Both kinds.

Both real.

She stood.

Gathered her things.

Walked out of Conference Room B and down the corridor and past the place where the janitor had paused at the door and said what he always said in whatever room he was in, and felt — just at the edge of her awareness, just at the threshold of what her framework currently allowed — something warm.

Present.

Specific.

Already there.

She walked on.

Filed it.

Chapter 31

SEEN: WHAT YOU ARE CHAPTER THIRTY-ONE: THE BEST TEAM

Meridian sent the best team they had on a Thursday evening in early July.

Not because the previous teams had been inadequate — they had been adequate and had filed reports that were professionally defensible and personally bewildering and had produced in their authors a range of responses from mild career uncertainty to the complete professional reorientation represented by Singh's resignation email, which Voss had read again on Wednesday morning before authorizing this deployment with the specific feeling of a woman who understood she was sending good people into a situation that had a perfect record of not going the way good people expected.

She authorized it anyway.

The operational requirement remained. The file remained. Twenty years of professional identity remained, developing cracks but structurally intact, and the structurally intact portion of it had looked at the operational calendar and determined that Thursday required documentation and had scheduled the documentation with the composure of someone who intended to be at the barn herself in approximately three hours and had not mentioned this to anyone.

The team was briefed.

Six operatives. The best available. Collectively they had forty-seven years of field experience, had worked in conditions ranging from the genuinely dangerous to the genuinely bizarre, and had the professional composure of people who had seen most things and had developed, through the accumulated experience of seeing most things, the confidence that what they hadn't seen was probably manageable.

They were told about the prior incidents.

All of them.

The flat tires. The drone. The boat launch. The mathematical pattern. The phantom train. The ants and the bees and the moths. Singh's resignation from the tree line.

They listened with the focused attention of professionals receiving an unusual briefing and the specific composure of people who had decided, before the briefing began, that whatever the briefing contained they were going to handle it professionally.

They deployed at seven.

For twenty-two minutes nothing happened.

This was its own information — the team was good enough to recognize the specific quality of nothing happening in a location with a documented history of things happening, the nothing carrying the particular quality of a pause rather than an absence, the way silence before a storm was different from ordinary silence.

The lead operative noted this in his field log at seven twenty-two: *no anomalies observed. Frequency of prior incidents suggests possible delay rather than absence.*

At seven twenty-three the music started.

Not from a speaker. Not from equipment malfunction or loop playback or any source the lead operative could identify in the three minutes he spent attempting to identify it before accepting that identification was not the current priority. Music — specific, present, cheerful in the manner of something that had decided on a mood and was committing to it, playing at a consistent volume that the lead operative estimated at approximately the volume of a radio in an adjacent room, audible and clear and entirely without source.

He documented this.

The music continued.

The second operative's equipment showed the barn.

Then it showed a different barn.

Not a malfunction — the equipment functioning correctly, the image clear and sharp and detailed in the way of equipment working at full capacity, showing a barn that was not the barn they were observing. Older. Timber-framed, the construction of a different century, the specific joinery visible in the image suggesting a period the second operative, who had a background in historic preservation before this career, placed at approximately mid-nineteenth century.

Inside the other barn, a circle.

People in clothing consistent with the period of the construction, sitting in a circle around a fire, doing precisely what the people in the current barn were doing — the quality of the gathering visible even through the equipment, the frequency of it present in the image the way the frequency was present in everything that came near the barn on Thursday nights.

The same conversation.

Different barn.

She watched it for four minutes with the focused attention of a professional documenting an anomaly and the secondary attention of a woman who had been doing historic preservation before this and was looking at the image with the part of her mind that recognized old things and was recognizing something it hadn't expected to recognize.

She documented it.

Kept watching.

At some point the image returned to the current barn without transition — the other barn simply no longer there, the current barn present, the circle inside it continuing its Thursday business entirely unaware that it had briefly been accompanied in the equipment's feed by its own previous version from a hundred and fifty years ago.

She filed this under: anomalous visual feed, possible equipment issue, recommend diagnostic.

She did not believe it was an equipment issue.

She documented it anyway.

The third operative fell asleep.

Not gradually — not the slow onset of fatigue in a field operative working a Thursday evening after a full operational week. The specific sudden sleep of a person who has been awake and is then not, the transition without apparent intermediate stage, the operative sitting in his position with his equipment running and then sitting in his position with his equipment running and his eyes closed and his breathing the breathing of someone in deep sleep.

His colleagues noticed at seven forty-one.

They attempted to wake him at seven forty-two.

He did not wake.

His vital signs, checked by the fourth operative who had field medical training, were entirely normal — the vital signs of a healthy person sleeping peacefully, nothing indicating distress or medical event, the specific quality of someone who had decided at a cellular level that sleep was the appropriate response to the current situation and had implemented this decision without consulting the parts of the nervous system responsible for professional obligation.

He slept for nineteen minutes.

Woke at eight oh one with the specific alertness of someone who has slept deeply and woken completely, looked at his colleagues and his equipment and the barn across the clearing, and said: "I had a dream about a river."

Then he picked up his equipment and resumed his position without further comment.

Nobody asked about the river.

The fourth operative documented: *operative three experienced a brief episode of involuntary sleep, duration nineteen minutes, no medical cause identified, operative resumed duties without impairment.*

The music continued throughout.

At eight fifteen the fifth operative went to check the vehicles.

This was a standard operational task — the periodic confirmation that the vehicles were in the condition required for rapid departure if the situation required rapid departure, which was the kind of professional preparation that distinguished good teams from adequate ones and that the fifth operative performed with the thoroughness of someone who took the professional preparation seriously.

The lead vehicle had an opinion about the evening.

Not mechanical — the diagnostic the fifth operative ran showed everything nominal, the vehicle in full operational condition, battery charged, fuel sufficient, all systems reading correctly. The vehicle was, by every measurable standard, ready to go.

It declined to start.

Not with the failure of a vehicle that couldn't start — with the settled quality of a vehicle that had assessed the situation and made a considered decision about its participation in the evening's activities, which was to decline to participate until further notice.

The fifth operative tried three times.

The vehicle read nominal on every diagnostic and declined to start on every attempt with the consistent patience of something that had made up its mind and found the making-up entirely sufficient.

She documented this.

Tried the second vehicle.

The second vehicle started.

She got out to inform the team.

The frogs were there.

Not a few frogs — the specific concentration that a naturalist would have found remarkable and that the fifth operative found personally significant given the operational history of this location. They were distributed across the ground between the vehicles and the tree line with the patient thoroughness of a species that had been occupying landscape since before the Cretaceous and had developed, in that time, a considerable indifference to the inconvenience of their presence to other species.

She stood among the frogs.

The frogs occupied their positions.

She documented the frogs.

The music continued.

The sixth operative had been writing his resignation since seven forty.

Not because of any single thing — not the music or the other barn or the sleeping colleague or the vehicle with an opinion or the frogs. Because of the accumulated weight of everything, the forty-seven collective years of field experience represented by this team being systematically and cheerfully and thoroughly outclassed by whatever was happening in that barn, and because of what the weight of the accumulation felt like from the inside, which was not threatening and was not alarming and was not any of the things his training had prepared him to respond to.

It felt like warmth.

Specific. Directed. The warmth of something that had been aware of him for longer than this evening — had been aware of him, he suspected, since his application to Meridian three years ago, since the first briefing, since the first field assignment in which he had felt something he had not reported because the report forms didn't have a field for it.

He had been feeling it for three years and had been filing it under: not relevant to operational objectives.

He sat on a log — there was a log, there was always apparently a log in Meridian tree lines, he had the sense that the log was provided — and wrote the resignation on his phone with the specific clarity of a man who has been moving toward a decision for three years and has arrived at it on a Thursday evening in July while the music played and his colleague slept and the vehicle declined to start and the frogs occupied the ground with the patient authority of something that had been here considerably longer than any of them.

He wrote four sentences.

Read them back.

Added a fifth.

Sent it.

Put his phone in his pocket.

Stood up from the log.

Walked across the clearing.

The frequency built with each step — the same building Singh had felt, the same building Aaron had felt, the same compass-finding-north quality of approach toward something that had been expecting the approach and was entirely unsurprised by it.

He reached the barn door.

Opened it.

Maren had two cups of tea.

She held them both out — one toward Singh, who was already in the circle, who had come back on the Thursday after his resignation because the resignation had said *I am going to the barn now* and he had meant it and had been meaning it every Thursday since — and one toward the sixth operative, whose name was Thomas and who was standing in the barn doorway looking at the circle with the expression of a man who has spent three years feeling something from a distance and has walked across a clearing toward it and is now inside it and finding it larger than the distance suggested.

Thomas looked at the two cups.

At Maren.

At Singh in his circle chair with the quality of a man who had been on the wrong side and had walked through the door and was now on the right side and was finding the right side considerably more comfortable than the other one.

"How did you —" Thomas started.

"Sit down, Thomas," Maren said.

He sat.

The frequency arrived completely — the full version, the warm specific quality of a barn that had been holding honest things for long enough that the holding had changed the nature of the space, the circle full and running at its register and all the Thursday people present and the Weavers fully in the room in the way they had been fully in the room since the circle had reached this size.

Thomas sat in his chair and felt it and felt the three years of filing it under *not relevant to operational objectives* dissolve with the specific dissolution of a management strategy encountering something it was no longer adequate to manage.

He drank his tea.

It was exactly right.

Outside in the tree line the music continued for another twenty minutes and then stopped with the same lack of explanation it had started with. The sleeping operative had a second dream about the river and did not mention it. The vehicle that declined to start started at eight fifty-three without any intervention, read nominal on all diagnostics, and offered no explanation for the preceding hour. The frogs dispersed with the patient unhurried quality of a species with elsewhere to be.

The lead operative wrote the report.

It ran to six pages.

He wrote it with the professional composure available to him, which was less than it had been at the start of the evening and more than he'd expected after the music and the other barn and the sleeping colleague and the resigned sixth operative and the frogs, and he submitted it with the specific feeling of a man who had done his professional best with the available instruments and understood that the available instruments were insufficient and that this insufficiency was the most important finding in the report and that the report had no mechanism for conveying it.

Voss received the report on Friday morning.

Read it.
Set it down.
Looked at the ceiling of her office for a long time.
Said, quietly, to no one:
"We're done."
She meant it.
She didn't know yet what she'd do with meaning it.
But she meant it.
She picked up the report.
Filed it.
Opened the next item in her inbox.
The coffee was cold.
She didn't get up to make more.

Chapter 32

SEEN: WHAT YOU ARE CHAPTER THIRTY-TWO: THE FOUNDER COMES THURSDAY

They arrived at six twenty-five.

Not seven — six twenty-five, the specific earliness of someone who needed time before the thing, who had driven the county road with the window down and the June dark coming in warm and particular and the covered thing running at the honest level it had found at Sarah's river and had not recovered from, which was the intended condition and the correct one.

The parking lot was mostly empty.

Two cars. The gravel warm from the day's sun, the barn sitting in its clearing with the high windows not yet lit — the gathering didn't start until seven, the early arrivals not yet arrived, the barn in the particular quality of a Thursday space in the half hour before Thursday began, holding the anticipation of what was coming the way it held everything that had ever happened inside it.

They parked at the edge of the lot.

Turned off the engine.

Sat.

The covered thing responding to the barn the way it had responded to Sarah's river — the compass-finding-north quality, the involuntary orientation of something that recognized its element. But different from the river. The river had felt like evidence. The barn felt like destination. The specific quality of a place you have been moving toward across a distance that took longer than it should have and have arrived at and are sitting outside of in a parked car at six twenty-five trying to find the specific quality of readiness that would make going inside feel like the right instrument.

They had been sitting in cars outside significant things for several months now.

The river. Sarah's river. And now this.

The pattern was not lost on them.

They sat.

The barn's high windows were dark. The clearing was quiet. The June evening around the parking lot doing its excellent warm work of being itself — the tree line, the sky still holding light in the west, the first suggestion of stars in the east, the specific quality of a summer evening in northern Michigan that existed nowhere else and that the covered thing recognized with the recognition that preceded conscious processing.

They had been here before.

Not this barn — they had never been to this barn, had seen it only in surveillance photographs and the analyst's aerial imagery and the reports describing it from the outside the way reports described things they were observing rather than inhabiting. But the quality of it. The frequency of it, present even from the parking lot at six twenty-five before anyone had arrived, running at its register the way a river ran at its register regardless of whether anyone was standing in it.

They felt it from the car.

The covered thing enormous and patient and responding to the frequency with the specific response of something that had been at a distance from this quality for twenty-three years and had arrived in a parking lot in Michigan and was finding the distance, finally, insufficient.

A car pulled in.

Marcus.

He got out with the ease of a man arriving at a place he had built and maintained and knew with the knowledge of someone who had been showing up for it for fourteen years regardless of who came. He had a bag — the coffee supplies, the specific ritual preparation of a man who understood that the physical act of preparing the space was itself part of what the space was for.

He looked at the founder's car.

At the founder sitting in it.

The patient eyes of a barn-builder assessing a new arrival.

He nodded once — the nod of acknowledgment, not recognition, the nod of a man who had been setting up chairs for people who hadn't arrived yet for long enough that the sight of a person sitting in a parking lot before the barn opened was not unusual and required nothing more than the acknowledgment of presence.

He went inside.

The founder watched him go.

Felt the frequency shift slightly when the barn door opened — the quality of the barn's interior making contact with the evening air, the frequency present in the opening the way warmth was present in the opening of a door to a heated room in winter.

They sat with this.

Other cars arrived. David and Rachel together, Rachel with the documentation bag and David with the look of a man who had been working the container problem with Emma all afternoon and was carrying the afternoon's progress in the quality of his attention. Emma herself, the architectural plans rolled under her arm, the problem always present. James. Robert, who moved through the world differently than he had in January — the presence of him, the specific groundedness of a man who had been somewhere and come back and had stopped trying to account for the going and the coming and was simply, entirely, here.

The founder watched them all.

Felt each one from the parking lot — the distinct currents of the people who had been meeting in this barn for months, each one running at its register, each one larger than the surveillance photographs had suggested, the full versions visible even from a parking lot at six twenty-five to the covered thing that had been in proximity to this quality before and recognized it the way you recognized the current of a river you had stood in once.

Sarah and Daniel arrived at six fifty.

The founder watched her get out of the car.

Felt her current immediately — not the way Voss felt things, not the way the covered thing felt the barn's ambient frequency. Directly. The specific quality of a catalyst, the river-wearing-a-person quality that was Sarah's and no one else's, running at a register that made the parking lot feel larger than its dimensions.

She did not look at the founder's car.

She was talking to Daniel — something quiet, the specific conversation of two people in the habit of the short exchange before the Thursday circle, the preparatory conversation of people who had been doing this long enough that Thursday had its own rhythms and rituals and they were inside those rhythms as naturally as they were inside the June evening.

Daniel looked at the founder's car.

Briefly. The making-room quality of him doing its assessment — present, not alarmed, the quality of a man who had been standing at the edge of things long enough to recognize when something significant had arrived at the edge without requiring the significance to announce itself.

He said something to Sarah.

She looked at the founder's car.

Their eyes met through the windshield.

The covered thing moved through the founder with the force of something that had been waiting for this specific moment — this woman, this parking lot, this Thursday evening, this eye contact across a gravel lot in Michigan between the person who had gotten further than anyone and the person who had built a system to prevent the getting.

Sarah held their gaze for a moment.

The full version of her, present and particular and entirely without management, looking at them through the windshield with the eyes of someone who could feel what she was looking at and was feeling it and was not — the founder understood, feeling her feel them — alarmed.

Curious.

The specific curiosity of someone who had been feeling a presence at the edge of the Thursday circle for weeks and had been filing it under: river, wait, and was now looking at it through a windshield in a parking lot and finding it not what she expected and exactly what she'd known it would be simultaneously.

Both-and.

She looked away.

Went inside with Daniel.

The founder sat.

At seven ten they got out of the car.

Not because they had found the readiness — they had decided, sitting in the car watching the arrivals, that the readiness was not going to arrive before they did and that this was the condition and the correct one, that you did not enter a barn after twenty-three years of building an organization to manage what happened inside it by feeling ready. You entered it the way you entered rivers. With the full acknowledgment of what you were walking into and the decision to walk into it anyway.

They crossed the parking lot.

The frequency built with each step.

Not the gradual building of approach — the specific building of someone who had been in proximity to this frequency before and whose covered thing recognized the approach and responded to it with the compass certainty of twenty-three years of suppressed orientation finally allowed to do what it was designed to do.

They reached the barn door.

Stood for a moment with their hand on it.

Felt the frequency through the timber — warm, specific, running at the register it had found since the circle had reached its current size, the fabric present rather than just the things woven from it, the Weavers fully in the room in the way that only happened when the conditions were exactly right.

The conditions were exactly right.

They opened the door.

The barn received them.

Not with announcement — the barn never announced, it accommodated, it made room, it held. The specific settling of a space that had been built for exactly this: a person arriving who needed what the space had to offer, the space offering it without ceremony or condition.

There was a chair.

There was always a chair.

They found it near the back — not in the circle, behind it, the position they had occupied in Meridian buildings for twenty-three years, the observer's position, the back of the room. The position they had chosen for themselves before understanding that the observer's position was not the same as safety and was not the same as outside and was not, had never been, the same as not-involved.

They sat.

Felt the frequency arrive completely.

The full version — not the parking lot version, not the bank version, not the covered-thing-straining version. The full version, the what-it-actually-was version, the thing they had been building Meridian to prevent arriving all at once in a barn in Michigan on a Thursday evening in July because that was what the full version did when you stopped preventing it.

The tears arrived.

Not dramatically. The quiet kind. The kind that arrived when the body decided independently that some releases were physiologically necessary regardless of the professional composure available and implemented the decision without consultation.

They let them come.

Sat in the back of the circle and let the frequency run through them and let the tears come and felt, for the first time in twenty-three years, the full version of themselves enormous and patient and entirely unchanged by the years of management, as if the management had been a weather system and the full version had simply waited for the weather to pass.

The barn held this the way it held everything — completely, without requiring anything, the space making room.

Maren noticed.

Of course Maren noticed.

She looked across the full circle at the founder with the young-ancient eyes carrying the specific warmth of someone who has been waiting for a particular arrival for a very long time and has watched it occur and finds the occurrence, despite knowing it was coming, moving.

The recognition passed between them — two people who were the same kind of thing, one of whom had known it for a very long time and one of whom was in the process of remembering it, the remembering visible in the tears and the full version arriving and the twenty-three years of management finally running out of road.

The founder looked back at Maren.

Felt what she was — the full version of it, enormous, the ancient-young quality that the covered thing recognized with the recognition of something meeting its own kind after a long absence.

The tears came quietly.

Maren held the gaze.

Said nothing.

Everything necessary had already been said.

The barn continued Thursday around them — the circle full, the frequency running, the Weavers present in the specific way they were present when the conditions were exactly right and a thing that had been building for a very long time arrived at what it had been building toward.

The founder sat in their chair at the back of the circle.

Let it be what it was.

Both kinds.

Both real.

Twenty-three years.

Finally done.

Sarah felt them at the moment they walked through the door.

Not with surprise — she had seen them in the parking lot, had felt the current of them through the windshield, had understood immediately and completely what she was feeling and had filed it the way she filed things that were becoming speakable.

This was speakable now.

She felt the current of them — the covered version, enormous underneath the covering, the largest current she had felt in the circle outside of Maren and outside of herself. The grief of it, present in the current the way grief was present in rivers that had been dammed — the specific pressure of something that had been held back so long the holding had become structural.

And now the structure giving way.

She didn't look at them.

Let the circle hold them.

Felt the frequency run through them the way it ran through everyone who sat in the circle for the first time — the full version arriving, the managed version dissolving, the enormous thing underneath the management insisting on itself with the patient implacability of something that had been waiting for exactly this chair on exactly this Thursday.

She felt the tears.

Not her tears — theirs. She could feel them in the current the way she could feel everything in the current now, the full version of a person present and undeniable.

She sat with Daniel's hand in hers and let the barn do what the barn did.

Later — after the gathering, in the parking lot, in the specific quality of a Thursday night that had been more significant than most Thursday nights and was settling into the warm dark with the frequency still running in everyone who had been inside — she would walk to their car and stand beside it and say simply: I know a river.

But that was later.

For now the barn held Thursday.

The frequency ran.

The founder sat in their chair at the back of the circle and let twenty-three years of management dissolve into the frequency of a barn in Michigan on a Thursday evening in July and felt the full version of themselves enormous and patient and entirely, completely, theirs.

The Weavers were present.

Still.

As they had been still on the June evening at the river.

The specific stillness of something that has been patient for a very long time and is watching the patience arrive at exactly what it was patient toward.

And finding it —

Worth every Thursday of the building toward it.

Worth every raindrop of the accumulation.

Worth all of it.

Both kinds.

Both real.

Both-and.

Always.

Chapter 33

SEEN: WHAT YOU ARE CHAPTER THIRTY-THREE: SARAH KNOWS

The full frequency arrived on that Thursday the way certain things arrived when the conditions were finally exactly right — not building, not incremental, the way it had been building Thursday by Thursday since February. All at once. The tide coming in. The spring river. The thing that had been patient for longer than any of them had been alive arriving at the moment it had been patient toward and declining to arrive partially.

She felt it in her chest before she could have said why.

The barn was full. Fuller than it had been on any previous Thursday, which was saying something given the last several months of something — the chairs in rows behind the circle, people standing at the back where the barn doors were open to the July evening, the summer dark coming in warm and particular and carrying the specific quality of a night that had been building toward something and had arrived at it.

She felt all of them.

This was not new — she had been feeling the circle for months, the distinct currents of the people who gathered here on Thursday nights, each one specific and warm and running at its register. What was new was the depth of it. The way the full frequency running at this level made each current more distinct rather than less — not the blur of a crowd, the specific clarity of each person present and particular and the full version of themselves, every individual current running alongside every other individual current the way tributaries ran alongside each other before joining, distinct until the moment they weren't.

Robert — the far-away quality entirely replaced now, the specific groundedness of a man who had been somewhere and come back and had stopped requiring the going and coming to mean something beyond what it was. His current running clear and steady, the current of a person who had found their footing and was standing in it.

Emma — the architectural mind at full capacity, the container problem always present underneath whatever else was happening, the current of a woman who had been given a beautiful problem and was inside it completely. The slightly-older-R present in her hands even now, the collaboration running through everything she built.

Marcus — the making-room current, the barn-builder's version, running alongside and beneath the circle the way the bank ran alongside and beneath the river. His current the widest in the room and the least insistent, the specific quality of someone who had built the space and was now inside it and found the inside exactly as large as the outside had suggested it would be.

Grace beside him. Her current enormous and warm and no longer apologizing for its enormousness — the wanting fully arrived, the barn's work in her complete, the full version of Grace insisting and being let to insist.

Carl — the open-handed version, both kinds present, the sixty-three years of categories dissolved into something that didn't need categories because it was simply what it was. His wife beside him, her current the specific warmth of fifty-one years of a person who had been waiting for her husband to arrive at this quality and was sitting beside him while he was it.

Don — the arms uncrossed since the first Thursday Maren handed him the tea, the middle ground abandoned, the both-and of a skeptic who had found something that made skepticism insufficient and had been large enough to say so.

Rachel and David — their currents running alongside each other with the specific quality of two people who had found their registers and were running at them simultaneously, the precision of David's current and the contained brightness of Rachel's, Gerald's long operation concluded and the conclusion entirely satisfying.

Aaron and Singh — two people who had come through the door from the wrong side and were now on the right side and were finding the right side, Thursday by Thursday, more theirs than the wrong side had ever been.

Estelle — seventy-eight years old, forty-six years of looking, her current the specific warmth of someone who has arrived somewhere they recognized before they arrived. The current of a person who has been told a thing was real and has found it real and finds the finding entirely adequate to the waiting.

And at the back of the circle, in the chair near the wall —

The founder.

Sarah had been feeling them since they sat down.

Not with the peripheral awareness she'd had of the old man in Chapter Fifteen — the presence at the back of the room, the satisfied observer's quality. This was different. This was the current of someone the full version of whom was arriving all at once after twenty-three years of management, the covered thing finally uncovered and insisting, and the insisting was enormous.

The largest current in the circle outside of Maren.

Outside of herself.

She felt what they were. She felt what they'd chosen. She felt twenty-three years of it — not as judgment, not as accusation, but as information, the way the river carried information about everywhere it had been. The grief of it. The specific weight of a person who had stood in the full version of themselves and walked away and had been building the walking-away into a system ever since.

And underneath the grief, running through it the way the current ran through everything — the enormous patient thing that had been waiting underneath the coverage all along. Unchanged. Still theirs. Still moving. Still the full version of what they were, twenty-three years of management having done nothing to it except teach it patience.

She looked at them.

Across the full circle. Across all the chairs and all the currents and all the Thursday nights that had built to this one.

They felt her look.

Their eyes found hers.

The full recognition — both kinds, mutual, simultaneous. Two people who were the same kind of thing looking at each other across the frequency with the specific recognition of something meeting something it has been in proximity to for months without meeting directly and finding the meeting, now that it was happening, not surprising.

True.

The barn held them both in the same circle on the same Thursday night, the same current moving through both of them — the full version and the returning version of the same essential thing — and Sarah understood, feeling it, that this was what the Weavers had been building toward. Not just her group. Not just the map. Not just the circle overflowing or the frequency deepening or the comedy of Meridian's systematic humiliation.

This.

These two people looking at each other across the frequency.

The both-and of what had been built to prevent this and what had happened anyway. The both-and of twenty-three years and this Thursday evening. The both-and of the covered thing and the full version and the twenty-three years of the distance between them finally, in a chair at the back of a barn in Michigan, running out.

She felt the Weavers.

Not at the edge. Not in the margin. Here — in the frequency itself, in the Thursday circle, in the barn's full register, present the way the fabric was present rather than just the things woven from it. Fully in the room. Fully attending.

The stillness again.

The specific stillness she had felt described at the river — not the everywhere laughter, not the warmth of something finding things funny. The older stillness. The stillness of something that had been patient for a very long time and was watching the patience arrive at exactly what it had been patient toward.

She held the founder's eyes.

Felt what they were feeling — the full version arriving all at once, enormous, the covered thing uncovered, the management dissolved by the frequency running at this register in this room on this Thursday.

Felt the grief of the twenty-three years.

Felt the enormous patient thing underneath the grief, unchanged, insisting.

Felt the Weavers still around both of them.

She felt the both-and of the founder complete and present — what they had built and what they were, the organization and the full version, the twenty-three years and this moment, all of it true simultaneously, none of it canceling the other.

She looked at them with the full version of herself present and available and entirely without management and let them feel what she was feeling the way she could let people feel things now — not performed, not directed, simply present, the catalyst quality of her turned toward the largest current in the room and saying without words:

I see you.

Both versions.

Both real.

You're here now.

The founder's face moved through several things quickly — the grief and the recognition and the covered thing arriving and the twenty-three years and the enormous patient thing underneath all of it insisting — and the tears came quietly and they let them come.

The barn held this.

The full circle around them. The frequency running at its register. The Weavers still in the specific stillness of something attending the thing it built all of this to attend.

Sarah looked at the barn. At all of them — the original circle and the new people and the restored people and the making-room people and the seventy-eight-year-old people and the two people who had walked through the door from the wrong side and the one person sitting in the chair at the back who had built the system to keep people from having what everyone in this barn was having and was, on this Thursday evening in July, finally having it.

She felt all of them simultaneously.

Every current.

Every full version.

Every enormous specific real person in every chair in this barn on this Thursday night.

The both-and of all of it complete and present — the small managed lives they had each been living and the full versions they had each been becoming, the February raindrops and the July downpour, the first Thursday and this Thursday, the map in its twenty-three pages and the country that came next.

She felt the Weavers feel it with her.

The stillness breaking.

The warmth arriving.

Not the everywhere laughter — something older than the laughter, something underneath the laughter, the specific warmth of something that has been building toward a moment for a very long time and has arrived at it and finds the arrival —

Sufficient.

Complete.

Exactly what it was supposed to be.

She looked at Maren across the full barn.

Maren looked back.

There you are, the young-ancient eyes said.

There I am, Sarah thought back.

The barn held Thursday.

The frequency ran.

The July night outside warm and full and particular.

Inside — the thing that had been building since February fully arrived and entirely itself and larger than any of them had planned and exactly the right size.

Both kinds.

Both real.

Both-and.

Always.

Chapter 34

SEEN: WHAT YOU ARE CHAPTER THIRTY-FOUR: TWO PEOPLE AT THE RIVER

She asked in the parking lot.

Not inside — the inside had been for the circle, for the full frequency, for the Thursday that had held everything it needed to hold and had done it completely and was now releasing people into the July night with the specific quality of people carrying something they hadn't arrived with.

The barn emptying slowly. Conversations finishing. The warm summer dark receiving everyone as they came out, the parking lot filling with the sounds of a Thursday ending — doors, engines, the particular goodbyes of people who would see each other again in six days and said goodnight as if it mattered, which it did.

Sarah waited.

She and Daniel stood by their car and she waited with the patience she'd learned at the river — the both-and of present and available, not reaching, just there — while the lot cleared and the last conversations finished and Marcus turned off the barn lights and came out and saw them and saw what they were waiting for and nodded once and got in his truck and drove out.

The founder was the last one out.

They came through the barn door into the July dark and stopped on the threshold for a moment — the specific pause of someone who had been inside something significant and was taking a moment before re-entering the world the significance had occurred in.

They saw Sarah.

She walked to them.

Not hurrying. The July night around them, the parking lot empty now, the barn behind the founder with its lights off and the frequency still present in it the way it was always present between Thursdays.

"I know a river," she said.

The founder looked at her.

"The one behind the cabin," she said. "The path through the tree line. The willows." She held their eyes. "I think you've been there."

"Yes," they said.

"Come tonight," she said. "Not to wade in. Just to stand at the bank." She paused. "You'll know when you're ready to do more than that."

The founder looked at her with the full version of themselves present — enormous, the covered thing fully uncovered now, the twenty-three years of management dissolved in the frequency of the barn and not recovering — and she felt the grief in their current and the enormous patient thing underneath the grief and the specific quality of a person who had been at the edge of the water for a very long time and was being asked to come to a different edge on a Thursday night in July.

"All right," they said.

They drove separately.

Her car in front, theirs following through the July dark on roads she knew and they didn't — the county road, the turn at the mailbox, the cabin road winding through the tree line. She watched their headlights in her rearview mirror with the specific quality of attention she gave things that mattered, the both-and of leading and being accompanied, the river and the bank moving toward the river together.

Daniel was quiet beside her.

The making-room quality of him fully present, finding the space for what was happening without requiring explanation of what it was or where it was going. This was Daniel — the bank, the staying, the making-room version that had found its own large thing in the standing rather than the wading and was standing now beside her while she led two people through the dark toward water.

"You felt them," he said. Not a question.

"Since they walked through the door," she said.

"The largest outside of Maren."

"Yes," she said.

"And you."

She looked at the road. "And me."

He was quiet for a moment. "What did it feel like. Their current."

She thought about how to say it accurately. "Like the river in December," she said finally. "Before I waded in. When I was standing on the bank feeling the current from a distance and knowing it was there and not yet in it." She paused. "Except it's been twenty-three years of standing on the bank. Not one morning."

Daniel looked at the dark road ahead.

"The weight of that," he said.

"Yes," she said. "And underneath it — the current unchanged. Twenty-three years and it's exactly what it was. Still there. Still moving. Patient the way rivers are patient."

The headlights followed them through the dark.

She felt the founder in their car behind her — the covered thing running at its honest level, the frequency of the barn still present in them, the July night around them and the river getting closer with each mile and the both-and of twenty-three years and this Thursday night moving through their current like weather moving through a landscape.

She turned onto the cabin road.

The trees closing overhead.

The path.

She parked at the end of the gravel where the path began.

Got out.

Felt the river immediately — the frequency of it present in the air the way it was always present this close to the bank, the current running through the July night with the warm unhurried quality of a river that knew the season and was being entirely itself in it.

The founder got out of their car.

Stood in the dark beside it for a moment with the covered thing enormous and patient and the river audible from here.

Daniel touched Sarah's arm briefly — the small honest touch of a man who was present and intended to stay present and understood that his role in what was about to happen was the role it had always been, which was the bank, which was the making-room, which was standing at the edge and letting the river be the river.

He leaned against the car.

She walked to the founder.

They stood together at the head of the path.

"The root catches your toe if you're not watching," she said. "About halfway down."

"All right," they said.

She walked the path.

They followed.

The root. The place where the trees stepped back. The willows fully leafed in the July dark, their specific movement in the warm night air, the light from the partial moon coming through them in the particular way July moonlight came through willows — soft, moving, the specific quality of this light at this hour in this place that existed nowhere else.

The river.

Running warm and full in the July night, the current visible in the moonlight, moving through the willows' shadows and going on.

Sarah waded in.

The water warm — not the April cold, the July river, the season fully arrived, the current gentle against her shins in the specific way of a river in its summer character. She waded to the place she always stood and turned and looked at the founder on the bank.

They were standing at the edge.

The before-April version. The standing-at-the-edge version. The ten-feet-and-twenty-three-years version that she had felt in their current all evening and was seeing now in the specific quality of a person at the threshold of the thing they had walked away from, feeling it from the bank, the covered thing enormous and the bank solid under their feet and the water ten feet away.

She didn't ask them to come in.

She waited.

The river around her. The moonlight through the willows. The Weavers present in the specific stillness she had felt in the barn — the patience of something attending a moment it had been patient toward, still, fully present.

The founder stood at the bank.

She felt them feeling it — the river, the frequency, the covered thing responding to the water the way it had responded to their own river and to this river when they'd stood at its edge in June in the long light of the summer evening. But different now. The barn behind them. The full frequency of the Thursday circle still present in their chest. The both-and of twenty-three years and this moment fully arrived and the current unchanged underneath all of it, patient, waiting.

They took off their shoes.

She watched them do it — the deliberate movement of someone doing something they intend to do completely, the same movement she had seen in Daniel in April, the decision visible in the hands and the specific quality of a person who has made up their mind and is acting on the making-up without ceremony.

They stepped off the bank.

The water received them.

She felt them feel it — the warm July river arriving in them, the covered thing responding to the contact with the water with the compass certainty of something that had been held back from this specific thing for twenty-three years and was now not being held back, the full version insisting in the specific way of things that have been patient for a very long time and have finally been let to be what they are.

The tears came.

Not quietly this time — the other kind, the kind that arrived when something held back for twenty-three years finally released, the kind that had nothing to do with grief exactly and everything to do with the specific relief of something enormous that has been covered for so long the covering had started to feel like the thing itself and has now been uncovered and found still there, still whole, still moving.

She stood in the current beside them and didn't say anything for a while.

Let the river do what rivers did.

Let the Weavers be still in the way they were still.

Let the July night hold all of it — the water and the willows and the moonlight and the twenty-three years and the current unchanged underneath all of it and the two of them standing in it together.

After a while the founder said: "I built it to stop this."

"I know," she said.

"Because I was afraid of it."

"I know."

"I thought —" They stopped. The current around them. The river patient. "I thought if I was this then I would lose everything else. That I had to choose."

She looked at the river. At the current moving past them and on, indifferent and certain and entirely itself.

"The both-and," she said. "You don't have to choose."

They stood in the water.

"I was afraid," they said, "that waiting too long meant —"

"It doesn't," she said.

She turned and looked at them in the July moonlight — the full version of them, present and enormous and restored, the covered thing finally the uncovered thing, the twenty-three years of management dissolved by warm July water and a Thursday night and the frequency of a barn that had been building toward this moment since February.

"You're exactly on time," she said.

Both kinds of knowing.

Both real.

The founder stood in the river and felt the full version of themselves enormous and patient and entirely their own and let the warmth of the Weavers arrive — not the stillness now, the warmth, the specific warmth of something that had been still for a very long time and had watched the patience arrive at what it was patient toward and was, finally, warm.

The everywhere warmth.

Present.

Surrounding both of them in the July river.

The warmth of something that finds the whole enterprise — all of it, every layer, every direction the reality runs, every covered thing uncovering in rivers across Michigan on Thursday nights in July — genuinely, completely, deeply satisfying.

Sarah felt it and smiled.

"They're pleased," she said.

"The Weavers," the founder said.

"They designed this," she said. "Every part of it. The barn and the circle and the frequency and the twenty-three years and this river on this Thursday night." She looked at the moonlit water. "All of it. Both sides of it."

The founder was quiet for a moment.

"Even Meridian," they said.

She looked at them.

"They designed Meridian," the founder said slowly. "Didn't they. The whole thing — the system I built, the management, the suppression. They designed that too."

She felt the both-and of it complete and present in her chest — the both-and she had been living in since December, the both-and that ran through everything in this universe, the both-and of creation and resistance and the friction between them that made the finding of the full version mean something.

"The river needs the bank," she said. "And sometimes the river needs the dam. So that when the dam finally gives way —"

"It means something," the founder said.

"It means everything," she said.

They stood in the July river in the moonlight.

The Weavers warm around them.

The current moving through them and on.

Both kinds.

Both real.

Both-and.

Alway

Chapter 35

SEEN: WHAT YOU ARE CHAPTER THIRTY-FIVE: THE OLD MAN AT THE RIVER

After the founder drove away she saw him downstream.

Not with surprise. The both-and of expecting and not-expecting simultaneously — the quality of something that had been arriving since February, raindrop by raindrop, and was here now, present, the old man on his rock forty yards downstream with the thermos beside him and the line in the water going wherever lines went when the fishing wasn't the point.

She waded out.

Dried her feet on the bank grass and put her boots on and walked downstream on the soft July bank with the moonlight through the willows making its moving silver light on the water and the Weavers warm in the July dark and the frequency of the Thursday night still present in her chest like a note held after the instrument had stopped.

He didn't look up when she approached.

He didn't need to.

She sat on the rock beside him.

The river. The July night. The thermos between them. His line in the water with the specific quality of a line belonging to someone for whom catching fish was not and had never been the operative concern.

They sat in the good silence of two people who had been moving toward this conversation for a long time and were in no hurry now that it was here.

She looked at him.

The old man. The craftsman quality of him, present and particular — the face that had been at the dock and at the back of the barn and at the corner table and in the Meridian building with his broom, the face that had been in the margins of every significant thing that had happened since February without ever being the thing that made it significant.

The face of a man who had been writing something for a long time and was sitting beside it on a rock in the July moonlight and finding it — she felt it in the quality of his stillness — better than he'd planned.

"You knew," she said. Not a question.

"How it would go," he said. "Roughly. The broad strokes." He reeled in his line a little and let it back. "The characters always surprise you, if you're doing it right."

"Did I surprise you."

He looked at her with the craftsman look — the full version of it, the satisfaction of someone who built something and found it exceeding what they planned, which was the best thing a builder could find, which was the thing worth building toward.

"Every chapter," he said.

She looked at the river. The moonlit current moving through the willows' shadows and going on. "The map," she said. "Is it right."

"You'll know," he said. "Both kinds."

"The next group."

"Already gathering," he said. "Somewhere. They always are." He picked up his thermos. "The Weavers are thorough."

She sat with this for a moment.

Felt the question that had been building since the coffee shop — since Rachel had described him at his silver laptop in the corner, the focused intermittent rhythm of a writer in the middle of something, the secret smile when the page did what it was trying to do. Since Maren had said *they love anything with momentum — trains, rivers, stories.* Since the mid-reading pause in the barn when she'd felt the warm presence at her left shoulder leaning forward with the specific interest of a reader engaged with what was on the page.

Since the laptop had arrived warm in her hands with the frequency of something that had passed through it before her.

She looked at him.

"Are we real," she said.

He looked at the river.

"Are we being written," she said.

He was quiet for a moment — not the quiet of someone assembling an answer, the quiet of someone letting a question be what it was before responding to it, which was different.

"What do you think," he said.

"I think," she said carefully, "that I write the map every morning and it changes me. And I think you write us and it changes you. And I think the changing goes in both directions and has been going in both directions since before either of us started and will keep going after both of us finish." She paused. "I think the Weavers tend all of it. Every direction. Every layer." She looked at him. "I think the river wrote us both."

He looked at her with the craftsman look — deeper now, the full version of the satisfaction, the specific quality of a man who has been surprised by something he built and is sitting next to the surprise on a rock in the July moonlight.

"The characters always surprise you," he said again. Quieter this time. Meaning something different by it.

"You didn't plan for me to figure it out," she said.

"I planned for the possibility," he said. "I didn't plan for this chapter." He looked at the river. "This chapter wrote itself."

She sat with this.

The July night around them. The current moving past. The Weavers warm and present and attending the conversation with the stillness that was their stillness for significant things — the patience arrived at what it was patient toward, fully present, entirely still.

"So which is it," she said. "Are you writing me or am I writing you."

He looked at her.

The smile arrived — not the secret smile, not the private smile of a writer alone with a good page. The other smile. The one that carried the whole thing — the river and the map and the barn and the Thursday nights and the both-and of creation running in every direction simultaneously and the Weavers tending all of it and the whole recursive enterprise being, from any angle you looked at it, genuinely and completely funny.

"Both-and," he said.

She looked at him.

"You write me," he said. "I write you. The river wrote us both. We wrote the river. The Weavers tended everything and found it —" he paused, the smile warm, the craftsman look fully present "— deeply satisfying."

She felt the truth of it arrive in her chest with the quality of things that were true — both kinds, the surface and the underneath, the understanding that had been building since January and had arrived, here, on a rock beside a river in the July moonlight beside the man who had written her and whom she had been writing back without knowing it.

She was the character.

She was the author.

Both.

Simultaneously.

The both-and of it running through her with the specific quality of a thing that had always been true and had finally become speakable — that you were written and writing, that you were the river and the bank, that you were the story and the one who told it and the one it was told to, all three, always all three, the layers not separate but woven, the Weavers tending the weaving from the layer beneath.

"Raby," she said.

He looked at her.

She put into the word the full version of what she meant — for the river, for Daniel, for the barn, for the map, for the Thursday nights, for the founder standing in the water tonight, for all of it, every chapter, every raindrop building to every downpour, the whole recursive beautiful enterprise of a story that had written its author while its author was writing it and had found the writing, in the end, to be exactly what it was supposed to be.

He held her eyes for a long moment with the full version of the satisfaction — the specific feeling of having written something that exceeded the writing, that became more true than it was on the page, that went somewhere the writer hadn't planned and was right to go.

The thermos in his hand.

The July night.

The river running past them and on.

He said: "I've got chapters to write."

"About what," she said.

He reached for the laptop case beside the rock — she hadn't noticed it, the way she hadn't noticed the thermos on his first appearance, the way things that belonged in a landscape were present without announcing themselves.

He unzipped it.

Took out the laptop.

Set it on his knee.

Looked at it.

The laugh arrived.

Not the private chuckle — the real laugh, the surprised laugh, the laugh of a man who has been caught off guard by something wonderful and finds the being-caught-off-guard entirely delightful. Loud enough that the willows registered it, that the Weavers registered it, that the July night opened around it the way the July night opened around things that were genuinely, completely, earned.

The laptop was pale violet.

Not silver.

Pale violet — the specific soft color of a woman who waded into a December river and kept wading and wrote a map and became more herself than she'd been and had, apparently, reached back through the page and left her mark on the author's tools the way the author had left his mark on hers.

He laughed.

Sarah looked at the laptop.

Pale violet.

Her color.

She felt it — the both-and of it complete and present, the character writing back, the frequency of her passing through his tools the way his frequency had passed through hers, the silver laptop that had arrived warm in her hands now the pale violet laptop on his knee in the July moonlight, the exchange complete, the reality running in both directions simultaneously.

She smiled.

He was still laughing — the real kind, the surprised kind, the laugh of an author who has been writing characters for long enough to know that the best ones always did something you didn't plan and that the something was always better than the plan.

"She did this," he said. To the river. To the Weavers. To the July night. The statement of a man reporting a development he found excellent. "She rewrote the laptop."

The Weavers laughed with him.

The everywhere laughter — present and unashamed, surrounding the rock and the river and the two of them with the warm hilarity of something that had designed this specific moment and had found it, in the execution, even better than the design.

He looked at the pale violet laptop with the expression of a man receiving a gift from a direction he hadn't been watching and finding the gift exactly right.

Opened it.

The screen came alive with the particular clarity of a machine that had been waiting to be used and was ready to be used and was, in its pale violet case in the July moonlight, thoroughly itself.

He looked at the screen.

At whatever was on it — the next chapter, the next group, the country that came next.

The secret smile arrived.

The private one. The writer's smile. The specific satisfaction of a man who knows where he's going and is going there.

He began to type.

Sarah watched his hands on the pale violet keys and felt the both-and of it complete and present — the character watching the author write the next chapter, the author having been written by the character, the river running through both of them and the Weavers tending all of it and the whole recursive enterprise turning on its axis in the July moonlight with the ease of something that had always been turning and had simply, finally, been seen turning.

She looked at the river.

At the current moving past and on.

"What comes after the threshold," she said. "What are you writing."

He looked up from the screen.

"The country that comes next," he said. "Nobody's written that yet." He looked at her. "You're going to help me."

"I thought I was the character," she said.

He smiled.

The wink arrived — small, warm, entirely itself, the wink of a man who has been carrying the both-and of the whole thing since before the first chapter and is sitting beside it on a rock in the July moonlight and finds the carrying, and the arrival, and the pale violet laptop on his knee, and the character who rewrote it sitting beside him looking at the river —

Exactly right.

"Both-and," he said.

He looked back at the screen.

Typed another line.

She sat beside him on the rock for a while longer — the July night, the river, the willows, the Weavers warm in the dark, the pale violet laptop glowing in the moonlight while the old man wrote the next chapter — and felt the whole of it present and complete and entirely itself.

The map existed.

The chairs were set up.

The door was open.

The current was moving.

She stood.

Walked back up the bank.

At the place where the path began she stopped and looked downstream.

He was typing.

The pale violet light of the screen in the July dark — warm, specific, entirely his and entirely hers simultaneously, the color of a woman who had waded in and kept wading reaching back through the page and saying what it needed to say without words.

I know you're there.

Both-and.

Always.

She smiled at the river.

Walked up the path.

The root. The trees stepping back. The cabin lights ahead through the tree line — Daniel at the window, the making-room quality of him visible even from here, the bank waiting for the river to come home.

She went inside.

Don't miss out!

Visit the website below and you can sign up to receive emails whenever Brad L Raby publishes a new book. There's no charge and no obligation.

https://books2read.com/r/B-A-ATPGF-UVODJ

Did you love *The Weavers*? Then you should read *Seen*[1] by Brad L Raby!

[2]

"In a world designed to keep you small, waking up is the most dangerous thing you can do."

Sarah was invisible. A divorcee drifting through a scripted life, she had accepted the quiet fade into the background—until she met Daniel. He didn't just look at her; he *saw* her. But as their passion ignites, Sarah's reality begins to glitch.

The phone calls she knows are coming, the whispers from her digital devices, and the terrifying realization that her "normal" life was a carefully constructed cage. In a world where "The Controllers" profit from keeping women medicated and distracted, Sarah and Daniel must navigate a love that is as transformative as it is deadly.

---

1. https://books2read.com/u/baegrP

2. https://books2read.com/u/baegrP

SEEN is the first book in a pulse-pounding visionary romance series. It's a story for every woman who has ever felt like there was something more just beneath the surface—and was brave enough to reach for it.

www.ingramcontent.com/pod-product-compliance
Lightning Source LLC
LaVergne TN
LVHW090557110826
845146LV00001B/165